EYES ON YOU FOREVER

EYES ON YOU FOREVER

JULIANNA PINKHASOVA

atmosphere press

Published by Atmosphere Press

Cover design by Kevin Stone

atmospherepress.com

Dedicated to all the girls who chased after him.
We are all in this together.

1

JASON

It's been exactly five minutes in this hell hole of an eighth- grade classroom, and I already want out. My temptation to leave this dull place is only growing stronger by the second.

The classroom is mostly deserted since I'm one of the first people here. I'm not usually this early anywhere, so the rest of the class is slowly beginning to stroll in.

The room is cluttered with tons of irrelevant posters that nobody actually cares to read unless they are some nerds without any personality.

The desks in this class are organized into groups of four just like in my last year's class.

Back in seventh grade, we had these futile name tags on our desks, and clearly not much has changed.

This school has first through eighth grade since Fuerika is a small town and there aren't many schools close by to each other. I still feel as though we are treated like a bunch of fourth graders because we still have line ups, and everyone here carries a lunchbox. It's like being back in my first-grade classroom all over again. Regardless of what grade we are in, we always have one main teacher that has us do what elementary students do. We still do carpet time, which feels weird to be doing at my age.

It would be great to actually live a real middle school experience with lockers and a different teacher for each subject, but not in my case.

The sight of my name tag catches my eye. It is plastered at the top of my desk that says "Jason" in script bolded letters.

The background chatter starts to amplify as the classroom gets fuller.

Finally, a dark brunette-haired boy sits across from me at his desk. His name tag says, "Mark."

It's not hard to tell that he is one of those basic boring guys that derives enjoyment from gaming. I don't understand the hype about video games, and I don't really want to.

My interests actually have meaning to them because what I like to do gets me whatever I want.

Who needs virtual games when real life itself is a game but more interesting.

Mark is wearing an average gamer t-shirt that has video game symbols all over it. There's nothing unique about this kid aside from his nice, expensive-looking shoes. Seems to me like he's a spoiled brat, but I can't complain because so am I. My parents have been spoiling me with everything I want for a while now. I get everything I want whenever I want it, and that's how I like it. It's one of my biggest flexes that I don't tell anyone. I'm not the type to talk about myself to people because people can use my information for horrible deeds. Nowadays, nobody can be trusted, so I'd rather remain private.

The second I leave my home, I mentally remind myself to stay 'hidden.' That way I don't expose who I really am and what kind of trouble I'm truly capable of. If anyone finds out what I do, they'll totally freak out and push me away.

The last time I trusted my 'friend' with my secrets, he exposed them, and after that people didn't look at me the same anymore. Luckily, I haven't seen those people in a long time after planting thoughts in their heads to not get involved with me. I don't need their drama, and I'd rather not risk getting more people knowing the dark things I can do.

Two more girls fill in the remaining seats at our combined desks that form our table, leaving no open seats available. My surrounding space looks as though it's closing in on me. All the parents that are adding to the cluster and heat of this room aren't making settling into class any easier.

Suddenly, my surroundings blur away, leaving only one girl in my focus. Sitting across from me is her. The most ideal girl I've ever laid eyes on.

My sight is entirely zoomed in on only her.

There's something so captivating about her, and I've got this strange temptation to indulge every detail.

Absolutely nothing else matters at this moment but this person who I refuse to believe has any flaws.

I didn't know people this ideal even existed until now. She has these beautiful brown beady eyes that I can't help but get lost in. Her hair is neatly pulled together and banded into a high ponytail. Every particular feature of her is just perfect. I can't resist but notice her milky pale skin and her rosy round lips that shape into a slight pout.

My mouth is salivating just thinking about tasting her soft, plush lips. I can imagine they must taste like the sweetest strawberry tart.

It's such a shame that she doesn't notice my eyes locked into those gorgeous eyes of hers.

Agitation and restlessness surges through me as I can't wait for her focus to be shifted onto me.

How has she still not noticed me?

My heart isn't racing anymore, and my muscles loosen at the thought of feeling her hand. I want to feel and memorize every crease and line of her soft and delicate palms.

Her hands are so aesthetically dainty that I can watch them all day and not feel bored.

A single quick glance at her name tag tells me her name is "Rosie" in big bold script letters.

Wow... even her name is just as pleasing as her appearance. If only she could just look at me, I would light up so fast.

My thoughts get interrupted by flashes of light, blinding my view of Rosie.

A middle-aged man standing to the side of Rosie continuously snaps countless pictures of her. She covers her squinting eyes at the blinding flash that keeps going off into her face.

"I think that's enough pictures, Dad," she says as she uncovers her eyes with her hand.

I'm guessing her dad is her lifelong paparazzi that makes her feel like some celebrity 24/7. Damn it... I wish I could get that kind of attention. It's something I've always wanted for as long as I can remember.

Even though I get what I want all the time, it's like attention is the most expensive thing for me to afford. I need attention, but it's something that takes me so much effort to obtain.

Rosie turns to Mark and softly smiles.

"Mark! You are in Rosie's class?" her father chirps.

Rosie's father is just another level of peculiar. I don't get the point of asking such a dumb question... as if he can't tell that Mark is obviously in this class.

I understand sarcasm, but not this kind.

"Yeah? I don't think we've met," Mark's face is puzzled.

Rosie's dad lights up with eagerness while he watches Mark and Rosie.

"Rosie, meet your cousin Mark!"

Rosie's eyes expand in complete surprise.

"I just greeted your dad in the hallway, Mark. You were only a four-month-old baby the last time I saw you."

"Oh, actually?" Mark fakes a smile.

"But how? I've never seen him before," Rosie says, unsure.

I have to admit that eavesdropping on all this is worth it. Dang... That's news though. The fact that Mark and Rosie are cousins can give me an advantage! I mean... It's not like Rosie would be interested in her cousin. Right?

"I have to go to work, but I will see you after school, Rosie. I'll explain everything when you come home!"

Rosie exhales a huge sigh of relief as her dad, along with the rest of the parents, finally leave our class.

Rosie and Mark are smiling at each other until Mark breaks their awkward silence.

"I've never seen you in this school. Is this your first year here?"

"Nope. I've been here since the first grade, but I haven't seen you anywhere either. It's a pretty big school."

They both smile bigger, and Mark begins to say,

"It's cool that we get to sit together in class. Um. have you ever played Fortnight?"

Wow, I was right about Mark. Of course, he has to bring up video games as if it has any relevance to anything. I feel bad for Rosie... The fact that she is forced to sit next to this gamer moron is just sad.

"No, I'm not really into that kind of stuff. I'm more into writing poetry and stories. It's one of my biggest passions."

"NO WAY! Same, I love writing poetry too!"

What an absolute pathological liar. I can't help but roll my eyes at his pathetic lie. There's no way that this gaming numskull is actually into writing. I mean... it doesn't take rocket science to figure him out unless you are naive and ignorant. Rosie is most definitely naive, falling for Mark's manipulative tricks, and it's absurdly sickening. He's obviously making stuff up to impress Rosie.

"Really? Wow, that's amazing. Can I read some of your poems? I'm sure they are interesting."

Mark hesitates like a doofus, as usual. He should feel embarrassed at this point.

"Um, actually I don't write poems anymore. I just like um... reading them. Maybe you can share your poems with me instead."

He is ridiculous. I mean really absurdly ridiculous.

Somehow, Mark and Rosie are a few inches closer together than they were just a minute ago.

My blood is boiling just watching these two get comfortable with each other.

"Yeah, I'd love to share my poems with you. I left all of them at home, but I can try to bring them tomorrow if you'd like."

"Sounds great. I'm not actually into video games either, I... just thought that maybe you were into them, so I brought it up," Mark lies.

Rosie's cheeks turn as bright red as Mark's face would be if I smacked him for being a lying bastard.

"It's alright. I think it's cool if you are interested in Fortnight. My uncle is actually a huge fan of that game."

If I had the chance, I'd smack Mark till he cries. Like... Why the lies? I wouldn't be surprised if someone dropped him as a baby, causing his head to not function properly. Is lying the only way he can keep a girl interested? I feel satisfied imagining him suffering for taking my girl and lying directly to her face. I don't get how any person can tolerate him.

Hold on... is this really happening right now?... Rosie is totally crushing on this dumb Mark dude. I should stop this before this jerk leads Rosie on any longer.

"Mark? Is that how you pronounce your name?" I interrupt.

Rosie is finally looking directly at me with her purely innocent gaze. I really can't get enough of her. I wish I could grab her away from Mark. She doesn't belong with that lying fool.

"Yeah, you pronounced my name correctly. What is your name?"

"My name is Jason," I say in my most confident tone.

Rosie looks at me again, but with complete indifference. This is all Mark's fault. My desire to kick Mark in the face is growing stronger than ever. What's most annoying is seeing the most attractive girl I've ever seen slip away from me before I can even get to know her.

He can't just steal her away from me that easily. At this point, Rosie doesn't even make more effort to look at me anymore, and I can't blame her. Mark is just a very manipulative person that thinks he deserves someone as ideal as Rosie.

HE. DOESN'T. DESERVE. HER.

I shouldn't worry though. I've gotten my way every time, so why should this time be any different?

I know I can get Rosie to love me simply by doing what I do best. My biggest secret still remains a secret, which is why this process will be way too easy for me. Rosie will be mine; she just doesn't know it yet.

2

ROSIE

It's only my first day being an official eighth grader and my dad is already making me the center of everybody's attention. He has probably taken over fifty pictures of me by now.

I'm used to getting too much attention, especially from my parents. I'm the youngest in my family, so I'm seen as a priority compared to my sisters. It makes sense, though. My sisters are twenty years older than me, which makes me the 'baby' of my family. It feels awkward knowing that my sisters are old enough to be my parent. Aside from getting so much attention at home, I feel like I'm getting it here more than I want.

I can't be the only person that thinks it's weird for parents to be in our class on the first day at our age. Even though parents leave after a couple of minutes, it feels off. This happens every year, but we are finally the seniors of the school, yet we are treated like children. I wish we had more independence to be prepared for maturing into older ages. What I'm certain of is that the majority of students in our school are very immature, and I can definitely see why. This school is the reason many people here remain thinking like children longer than they are supposed to. Unlike most people, I'm mature, according to my family. I can't stand childish drama, and I prefer to mind my own business.

My face feels hot, and I can imagine my face probably looks like I'm wearing a hundred layers of blush. It doesn't help that the flash coming from dad's phone is all up in my face.

I told Dad I think he's taken enough pictures so this can be over with. I bet people were staring at us, and who knows what they could be thinking. I can't be putting on a bad impression before even trying to make a first impression.

Apparently, the boy that sits next to me is my cousin who I have never seen before. At least according to my dad, Mark is my cousin. Since I've never seen him before, I'm guessing we aren't related by blood, which can actually be such an advantage to me.

Mark seems so friendly, so if we aren't closely related, it wouldn't be so weird if we form a closer connection.

Either way, the fact that my seat was put next to his can't possibly be a coincidence. What are the odds that two related people are put in the same class and seated next to each other? Maybe the odds are high, but this seems planned. It's like the teacher knew about this, or I could just be overthinking like I do on first days.

I can tell from the corner of my eye, the boy across from me is deeply analyzing me.

It's probably because of my dad's photography shoot that's making me the spotlight.

Maybe there's something wrong with what I'm wearing? No, I doubt that... I put on my best outfit for my first day back at school.

I'll admit that maybe If I wasn't short on time getting to school, I would have chosen something more appealing to wear.

I'm never late anywhere, so I couldn't break that streak on the first day of eighth grade.

It just occurred to me that the boy sitting across from me doesn't seem all that concerned about what I'm wearing; he is mostly staring at my face. I doubt that he is zoning out... He's been taking interest in my face for far too long.

Slightly peeking at his name tag, I can see his name is Jason.

I've never met anyone with that name before, but I'm sure it's a common name.

Mark asks me if I am into Fortnight, and at that point Jason's eyes zoom in on Mark and me more attentively.

Should I be concerned?

He looks like he is about to erupt when he looks at Mark. Jason's hand is literally in a fist, and his knuckles look like they are about to pop right out of his hands. I can't tell if Jason realizes how hard he is squeezing out a fist.

Mark and I continue our conversation, and luckily, we share similar interests, which is incredibly fascinating. He says he likes reading poetry, and that's pretty convenient for me. I absolutely love writing in general, but poetry is always my number one. I'll probably start writing actual songs one day and get famous for it.

The fact that I've made a friend before class has the chance to start is amazing.

Every time I look at Mark, my cheeks feel like steaming hot tomatoes.

Jason introduces himself, so I finally look directly at him rather than from the corner of my eye.

Getting a closer look at him, I'm in disbelief. Although, showing more disinterest to not make it seem like I am judging him seems more appropriate.

Jason is actually small in height, and he looks really petite. I've never seen anyone like him, so he looks kind of funny to me. I can barely see the other half of his neck because he is sitting so low. His chair is high up, which is another plus to how short he is. We are both definitely similar in some ways aside from the fact that I am a few inches taller than him.

Looking around the class, me and Jason seem to be the only short and petite ones. He has such a high-pitched voice, and it makes me wanna burst into crying laughter.

Something about him is very hilarious to me, but I'd rather keep it cool for now. I can literally write an essay on why he looks like the funniest child I've ever seen. He kind of gives off girly playful vibes just by judging off his voice and appearance.

Our teacher finally starts the class. She is wearing a long brown cardigan with a tank top and jeans.

I swear every teacher has the same style.

I can imagine an entire meeting of teachers deciding on what their clothing attire should consist of. It's kinda silly, but I wouldn't be the least surprised if that's the truth.

"I would like all eighth graders to bring their attention to the front of the classroom. My name is Ms. Hendrick, and I can't wait to get to know you. Each of you has a piece of paper on your desk with your partner's name on it. These will be your partners for every time we meet to learn on the carpet. Now find your partner and sit with them on the carpet."

I hope Mark is going to be my carpet partner. I don't know anyone else in this class, but so far, I feel most comfortable with Mark. I don't know if Mark is interested in being friends with me yet, but I don't have major doubts. If anything, there are many others in this class that look kind of approachable. The girl that sits in front of me has been digging her nose for gold this entire time. I thought eighth graders were supposed to be mature, but here I can tell that I thought wrong. If she is my partner, then I'd probably dread partner work for the rest of the school year. I kind of feel bad for her, though. She's probably not gonna have any friends this year from being so gross. Not trying to be rude, but she's an eighth grader, yet she has no shame picking her nose in front of people. She also scratches her head a lot... it's like she's got lice. Whoever has to work with her is in for a treat, and I genuinely feel bad for them and her at the same time.

The imperfectly folded paper says a name I don't recognize at all.

"Tomas" it says.

I can relax knowing that the nose gold digger won't be my partner, but I hope Tomas isn't any worse than her.

I glance up for a quick few seconds, and Jason is already glaring at me. He's deeply examining my eyes like he's never seen a girl's eyes before. I can't tell if he's just trying to be funny or if he's actually serious. I'll start looking for my partner now before Jason makes things any more awkward.

3

JASON

We all got our partners' names, and I got some girl named Janice as my partner. Rosie just opened her folded paper, and her perfect face barely displayed any reaction. I have high hopes that Mark isn't Rosie's partner. The thought of it makes me want to punch him really hard. After all, he really would deserve it. He is such a lying jerk, and he's been pushing my buttons before class even started.

He has serious issues if that's the best skill he's got to impress Rosie. Besides, he is her cousin, so leading her on is the worst thing he can do. She needs a real man like me, not some pathological lying fool that only knows how to lie to keep a girl interested. I feel bad for Rosie having to be related to someone as insincere and fake like him. The feeling of jabbing my fist into his jaw makes my hands tingle. That would be one of the most pleasing sensations ever after hearing all the crap that came from his annoying mouth.

I can't resist not taking my eyes off Rosie just yet. I know

I should be looking for my partner, but that can wait. Right now, the main focus is finding Rosie's partner.

Whoever it is, I'm just hoping it isn't another boy, or we will have bigger problems. Mark looks like such an airhead looking around. It's not hard to tell that Rosie isn't Mark's partner. He's been searching and asking around like an idiot.

Almost everyone is on the carpet, but not him of course. Just thinking about another boy having Rosie's attention makes me want to smack every guy in this classroom. I know it would make me feel better. I've gotten physically violent before, and it felt very satisfying because I never lose a fight. People shouldn't underestimate me just because I'm short. If only they knew that I could damage them in ways that could potentially ruin their life eternally.

I can't give up the love of my life to some random jerk who doesn't deserve her.

In fact, I'm the only real man that she deserves and needs in her life.

Wow. Would you look at that? It's truly a miracle that Mark the doofus found his partner after taking forever.

Thankfully, Mark's partner is a random girl with long blonde hair. I don't need to worry about him for now.

Rosie, on the other hand is sitting in between two boys. One of them is fully blonde, and the other has hair as black as charcoal. I can't tell which one of those boys is her partner, but that's the least of my worries.

If any of those boys even dare to smile or enjoy her too much, I wouldn't mind knocking them out in front of everyone. They have no idea who they are dealing with.

I can't look away from them now... at least not until figuring out who Rosie's actual partner is.

At this point everyone is already sitting on the carpet with their partners except for me and the only other girl standing. The room goes completely silent, and thirty-two eyes are staring at me and Janice.

"Why are the two of you still standing?" the teacher scolds.

Rosie is looking directly at me with her adorable, innocent glance.

The teacher is literally embarrassing me in front of Rosie for the dumbest reason ever. I can't afford losing her now just because our dumb teacher feels like making me look bad. I could just punch her so hard, and it would feel so satisfying.

Ms. Hendrick has the nerve to raise the tension in the room for attention.

Janice and I finally sit with the rest of the class, and all eyes finally look back at the teacher.

Rosie is still glaring at me, and our eyes lock with each other's.

Can this be the moment she realizes she is in love with me? Nope, I can't get my hopes up this soon. Maybe she is still trying to learn about me the way I want to learn about her.

I need to know everything there is to know about her; that way I'll be the perfect guy in her eyes.

I'm sure that nobody – not even Mark or any other pathetic dude in this class – can take her away from me. I'm certain of this because I won't give up on what's mine.

When my parents buy me a new toy that I've always wanted, I don't give up on it the second I get it. I hold onto it because it's my possession. I wouldn't let anyone steal it even if I didn't need it anymore. The same goes with Rosie. The fact that I want her is the very reason I already claimed her.

I've got my eyes on you, Rosie, and any guy that even dares to steal you away from me will suffer very soon.

4

ROSIE

I'm finally seated with Tomas in the middle of the carpet, and I just wish I could stop all these thoughts from racing through my mind.

It is the first day, so this overthinking issue will be gone by tomorrow. I'm not an overthinker until the first day of a big change for me.

I swear, I have so many questions multiplying in my mind before I can even process them.

What if Tomas isn't the right fit to be my partner?

I can't afford working with irresponsible people, and I don't wanna dread working with him. This is literally the worst possible time I could be overthinking... but I can't help it. My past experiences were dreadful and disappointing. I get goosebumps on my arms just remembering them.

Last year, I was partnered with a group of people that all refused to work on assignments, so I ended up doing all their work for them all year long. It was draining me mentally and physically for the entire school year. I love learning, but that doesn't mean I should be learning for every student that's in my group.

It sucks that we can't choose our own partners, but that's unrealistic in the outside world. In the real world, I might be forced to work with colleagues I can't stand being around, but that's life, and I have to put up with it.

For some reason, the entire class including the teacher, faces the back of the classroom. They all seem to be staring at something or perhaps someone.

At this point, I shouldn't be surprised, but that strange kid Jason is standing in the middle of the room, glaring at me and the two boys sitting at my sides.

His hand is in a fist again, and he is squeezing his knuckles out harder than ever.

Oh my gosh... no way... Jason's partner is the nose gold digger that sits in front of me at our table. That really sucks for Jason, but I don't care. Maybe now he can stare at her for hours and leave me alone. He probably thinks it's funny, but it's really disturbing. If he has something he wants to say to me, why not just say it to my face?

My thoughts get interrupted by Ms. Hendrick's commanding voice scolding Jason and his weird partner to be seated on the carpet. He freezes there, just staring at me, probably lost in his own thoughts. I seriously don't get what is up with this kid. Is he trying to be funny again because it's not working.

After what seems like forever in this awkward silence, he takes a seat on the opposite side of the carpet from me. Before any further reaction, Ms. Hendrick takes a rapid breath in and says,

"Alright class, take the next few minutes to introduce yourselves and get to know your partners! Turn to face your partner and share some facts about yourself. Then we will share some facts we learned about our partners with the rest of the class."

If I hear her say the 'partners' one more time, I'll lose it. That's the impatience talking from the overwhelm. I'm very patient in general, and my family loves me for that. I can bear anything that comes my way... or at least everything I've experienced thus far.

This is just... great. The moment I've been overthinking for the past five minutes without a single break, Tomas turns his entire body to face mine. He clears his throat and...

"Hey um... I'm Tomas, but you already know that. And you're Rosie?" Tomas continues to avoid eye contact and fidgets with his fingers.

"Yeah, I'm Rosie."

Tomas finally looks up at me and smiles.

"Is it cool with you if I call you Rose? It just um... sounds like a nice nickname."

"Of course, I'm cool with that. It actually sounds cute... I like it."

Tomas's entire face lights up with a huge smile that almost reaches his ears.

I can tell Tomas isn't very calm right now, but I can't blame him. It's the first day, so everyone is going through it.

"So... tell me some interesting facts about yourself," he chuckles as he reddens even deeper.

"Well, I guess I'll start off with my biggest passion of all time. I absolutely LOVE writing with all my heart. It's like my getaway from reality, even though I love living in the moment too. OH! And speaking of living in the moment, I also love to travel and spend time outdoors. I'm also very passionate about cooking and OH I love getting creative with crafts! I also—"

"Damn. It sounds like you are very passionate," Tomas interrupts.

"Oh... I really am and sorry if I went overboard with talking about myself. It's just that I don't usually get the opportunity to talk about these things that make me happy."

"No, don't apologize. You sound like a very interesting person, and I can tell that working together will most definitely be fun and productive," he says.

I can't help but chuckle. Tomas is not what I was expecting. In fact, he sounds better than I expected, which is usually rare. I think it's kinda cute how we both can't stop smiling, but it's somehow comforting. We both get silent and just stare at each other; our smiles getting awkwardly crooked.

"How about you? I bet you have many interesting facts about yourself," I finally say.

"Ah, that's right, but not as passionate as you, that's for sure." Tomas clears his throat again and...

"Um... so My favorite food is sushi"—he laughs – "I'm also a huge fan of—"

Literally out of the blue, the teacher interrupts. "Alright boys and girls, please bring your attention back to the front. We are about to share what you learned about your partners."

Tomas and I exchange glances. I barely learned anything about Tomas aside from the fact that he is a sushi lover. Maybe if I didn't go on rambling about my passions, Tomas would've got the chance to introduce himself... and now I might embarrass him in front of the entire class if I get called on. Luckily, other students are sharing about their partners, which can actually buy me some time.

I spent so much time minding my own business that it just occurred to me that Jason is literally staring at me... and very intensely.

How long has he been glaring at me like that?

Was he focused on me this entire time?

"Tomas, you're up next! What have you learned about Rosie?"

Oh... this can't be good. If Tomas is going next, then that can only imply that I go right after him.

"Uh, so I actually call her Rose now, since that's the nickname we came up with for her."

The teacher's smile flickers across her face like a hologram.

"That's really sweet, Tomas. Go on."

Tomas's face lights up into bright tomato red. He clears his throat... again.

"I learned that Rosie is very passionate about writing, cooking, traveling and getting creative. She loves spending time outdoors and living in the moment. I really value this about her, and I think she is really cool for that. I feel special now that I made friends with such a passionate girl."

Wow... I'm mostly speechless. Tomas is such a sweetheart and I– Ms. Hendrick's voice barges right into my thoughts.

"Rosie, what have you learned about Tomas?"

Tomas made me look so good, and I'm about to let him down. I wish time could just fly at this point. I take a deep breath in. Alright, here I go.

"Well, Tomas is um... a sushi lover, and he also has a very bright personality. I didn't get to finish hearing him express himself because the teacher stopped us too early but—"

Ms. Hendrick raises her eyebrows.

"I gave you plenty of time to speak with your partners and everyone else that shared out, all learned a lot in those few minutes. You should've been more prepared."

Ms. Hendrick moves on to the next student, leaving me feeling like crawling into a hole and just lying there in emptiness. I'm not too great with being scolded by teachers. I never really understood why they love reproaching students so much. Jason is still glaring at me, but that's not news.

What's the matter with him?

I don't mean to whine, but this hasn't been the first time today that Jason has been staring into the depths of my soul.

Tomas looks down to the floor, lost in his own reality. I think this will all be forgotten by tomorrow, so it shouldn't matter much longer... hopefully.

5

JASON

I have to admit that being partnered with Janice really dis-rupted my lookout for Rosie and her pathetic partner.

So far, everyone is introducing themselves to their partner, and I let Janice go first. Although I am tuning out Janice and her dumb stories about her annoying self, it's all worth it. Janice actually sits next to me and in front of Rosie at our desks. That really sucks because she picks her nose occasionally when she is talking about herself to me. Her nose isn't the only thing she's been digging, but her hair too. This is literal proof that no girl is as perfect as Rosie. Janice's voice is so irritating to listen to. It's like listening to a cat's claws scratch across a chalkboard. I can't wait for her to shut up already.

There she is, my beloved Rosie, sitting with that moron who deserves a good beating to the head. Maybe knocking some sense into that spud head would teach him to back off from what's mine.

Rosie's entire body is facing her partner, so my only view

of what's happening is Rosie's back and her partner's brittle face. Just imagining myself uncontrollably kicking him in the face is excessively satisfying. I don't see myself as an angry person; I'm just protective of my belongings, which is fair. I have every right to feel the way I feel towards guys that talk to Rosie because they didn't ask for my permission to speak to her. Regardless of if they would ask, I would say no to them anyway.

The way her partner looks at her so attentively is just revolting! This bastard reddens the longer he stares at her.

He's nothing but a pathetic creep that should be put back in his place.

What if he's making my Rosie uncomfortable?

I should be protecting her from this creep. Who knows what kind of crap he's capable of.

Janice is staring at me... I guess waiting for me to talk now that she's done blabbing about her annoying life. I let out a deep sigh in hopes that I don't seem like I'm about to literally explode and go off on Rosie's partner. Thankfully, the teacher stops us all just in time and I don't have to waste a single second of my attention on useless Janice.

Rosie is finally facing in such a direction that her face is much more visible to me. Her face is so pure and angelic. Looking at her face makes me feel so full of life. I can't resist but wonder what her milky porcelain skin tastes like.

I want to feel her... taste her... I want all of her. That doesn't make me a creep because I simply just want to enjoy the love of my life like any normal person would.

Honestly, I've had enough of all these brainless morons stealing her away from me. By the end of the day, I'll make sure I have her right where I want her. Otherwise, who else will protect my sweet Rosie from all these creeps?

Rosie's partner got called on to talk about my Rosie, and I can't even begin to express just how badly I want to strangle the crap out of him! THIS CREEP GAVE MY ROSIE A NICKNAME!! 'Rose,' is how he referred to her. Rose... MY Rose.

Rosie is all smiley, watching as he talks about her passions to the class. I can't tell if I want to drain my eyes out with my tears or scream from the top of my lungs. I gotta stop myself... I can't get distracted, as this is the perfect opportunity to learn about my beloved Rose. This moron will get what he deserves, so the thought of it soothes me.

So far, I'm just making my mental list of Rosie's passions. These will be very useful to me later on.

My Dear Rosie's passions:

- *Writing*
- *Cooking*
- *Traveling*
- *The outdoors*
- *Getting Creative*

Rosie is up next talking about her partner and our dumb teacher just scolded her even though Rosie did nothing wrong. If there is anyone in this class worthy of suffering besides these morons, it would definitely be Ms. Hendrick. This woman offended me and is now offending my sweet Rosie. Ms. Hendrick makes me want to smack her so badly. Who's the idiot that gave her a teacher's license? She doesn't deserve to teach a class, and if it weren't for me being focused on Rosie, I would work on getting Ms. Hendrick fired. It wouldn't be so hard anyway because I know that this is my world and everyone in it gets the privilege of living in it. I can take that privilege away just by desiring them to be gone. I always get what I want, and after I get enough information on all these idiots, I'll know the best ways I can eliminate them for good.

6

ROSIE

We are finally sent back to our seats after most of our class shared out about their partners. What's weird is that not everyone was called on to share out loud. I'm not complaining, though, because we get to do silent reading before lunch time. I choose the thickest book from the book bin that can keep me most entertained. I absolutely love reading. My passion constantly surges within me when I read or write. I've been like this for as long as I can remember, and It's such a blessing. I feel like the luckiest girl in the world because I have so many interests and passions.

Mark taps on my shoulder and points to the hilarious picture in his book.

"Look Rose, this girl with thick eyebrows looks like our teacher," he giggles.

I slightly giggle with him. I feel close to Mark, as if I've known him forever. We share a very similar sense of humor, which makes our bond much more interesting. I didn't realize it at first, but building a connection with Mark is happening sooner than I thought. He always smiles so passionately when he looks at me, which is very adorable.

Jason's hand is in a fist once again, but this time his skin is the color of a tomato.

Wow, Jason looks even funnier with all these hilarious faces he's making.

What's he getting so heated about anyways?

I place my lunchbox in Jason's view of me before his rage stare intensifies any stronger.

His pupils dilate bigger when he looks at Mark and me side by side. This tension between Jason and the both of us is really unnecessary.

It's ridiculous how Jason is holding his book upside down as though it hides the fact that he's staring at us. I don't actually care, and I mind my own business, but seriously... what sane person wouldn't question being stared at so much?

Maybe he's just bored? But there are a bunch of other students he can focus on, so I don't understand what he finds so interesting about Mark and me.

Jason stands up and walks by Tomas's desk and stealthily peeks at his name tag. Suddenly he goes on to sharpen his already sharpened pencil because he thinks he's slick. This is beyond comical... I can't imagine what goes on in his head.

Jason is sitting back at his seat across from me with a smirk plastered onto his smug face.

"Attention eighth graders, it's time for lunch! Line up in a single file line!" Ms. Hendrick shouts.

"Are you getting school lunch today?" Mark says as he shows off his beaming white smile.

"Probably not because I bring my own lunch from home. How about you?"

"Nah... I don't go anywhere near the school lunch," Mark snickers.

Tomas taps on my shoulder.

"Rose, can I save you a seat at lunch? I'm in the mood to talk some more, if you don't mind."

"Thanks Tomas! And yes, you can definitely save me a seat," I say, feeling giggly.

I could literally scream in jubilation if I had the chance...

OH. MY. GOSH... So far, I've made two friends, and I didn't even have to try.

Mark gives Tomas a black look, but Tomas doesn't seem to notice.

When Mark looks away, Tomas rolls his eyes at Mark.

What's with all the mysterious rivalry between the guys today?

It's like they all hate each other without even knowing each other.

I'm guessing it's just a guy thing.

Last year in the seventh grade, all the boys were neutral with each other for the most part. Not sure what's the deal with the boys this year, though. Regardless, I'm just excited for lunch time. I'm starving.

7

JASON

Inconveniently, Rosie has placed her lunchbox in the way of my perfect view of her face. I can always look at her from other angles, but she would get suspicious of me. After all, she doesn't understand that my undivided attention for her is to protect her from these morons. Soon she will accept this and all that I am planning to do to her and her pathetic guy friends.

After a quick stroll by Rosie's partner's desk, I got a glimpse of his name.

"Tomas." Such a basic name, but it definitely suits him for being the basic turd that he is. I am obviously more of a catch than charcoal-haired Tomas, who probably has no luck with girls. I mean, yeah... Sure Rosie may like this dude, but what I have planned for him will make all my worries gone for good. Tomas can barely speak to a girl without sounding like a nervous goofball. Either way, he still has no right to involve himself with my property. I claimed my beautiful Rose long before he did, so there's no way I will give her up to him or anyone else.

She was made for only me. Tomas of ALL people obviously doesn't deserve Rosie, and that's for me to judge.

Who gave this idiot the right to speak with her? It's not like I'd forbid him from breathing around her...

On second thought, I would. BUT that doesn't change the fact that he doesn't have the right to be her friend because next thing I know... he might even intend a relationship with my Rosie. I don't care what the teacher says, or what anyone says for that matter. This is my world, so I don't need these crappy guys going around stealing from me. Rosie doesn't realize just how precious she is. She can get taken from me at any given moment, which is why I can't afford to distract myself away from her presence.

Casually, I sharpen my pencil to eliminate any suspicions of me checking out Tomas's name tag. He really has no idea what's coming for him if he continues being the crackhead that he is.

Mark and Tomas are both talking to Rosie right now, which would be the perfect moment to kick them both where it really hurts, but I can't. Our teacher is watching our table like a hawk since Tomas isn't supposed to be at our table. What's really surprising is that Ms. Hendrick doesn't scold Tomas for not being at his seat. Yet when I was still standing with Janice during carpet time, she yelled at me. Getting Ms. Hendrick fired is definitely one of my goals on my mental bucket list.

Before I know it, we are putting our books away and getting ready for lunch time. This is my chance to actually get closer to my Rosie. This is the moment I wouldn't miss out on for anything.

8

ROSIE

My appetite is so big right now that I can eat everyone's lunch in this class and still not feel full. We are all lined up and following our teacher down to the cafeteria when suddenly I feel tickling sensations rolling down my back. It's like someone's hand is caressing my body. It's not impossible to tell that this person is walking way too close to me that I can literally smell their personal scent. Insanely odd chilly sensations and goosebumps grow on me as their hand softly glides down my forearm. I turn around with full speed and wow... should I be surprised? Jason, with the biggest toothy shark smile is glaring at me like I'm his long-awaited meal. My heart thumps louder as his eyes dilate, looking at my face. I pace up my walking as fast as possible in an attempt to flee Jason, but somehow, he manages to always catch up to me.

After what seems like an eternity, we've made it to our assigned table in the cafeteria. Even though Jason is seated far from me, it still feels like his eyes are all over me. I feel supervised by him at all times. Even my parents don't watch me with so much attention the way that he does. Like seriously, what does he want from me? I'm just glad I feel safe at my end of the table now that Jason isn't as close to me as he was five minutes ago.

My mom packed me the most delicious, buttered pasta and a turkey sandwich for lunch today. Although there is nothing wrong with what my mom packed for me, I'm getting on the lunch line just to be out of Jason's sight for a little while longer.

OH MY GOSH... I can't believe what I just witnessed. It's really an incredible miracle. Jason is finally distracted, which is my perfect escape to the lunch line before he notices that I'm gone. I literally sprint out of my seat and run to the end of the lunch line. I exhale the shakiest exhale I've had all day. I'm just glad that my skin is clearing from all the goosebumps. Looking back at my table from the lunch line, I see that Jason is no longer at the table. I feel my cheeks heating up and my palms sweating. Being paranoid at this moment is an understatement. I hurriedly look around the cafeteria with tears in my eyes, and there he is, standing on the lunch line. Lucky for me, Jason is standing behind the girl that is standing behind me. He is standing there watching me like a hawk. What if I just make a run for it? But where would I go? What would be my excuse? Instead, I speed walk off the lunch line, and Jason follows me back to our table. The fact that I'm stuck with this guy for the rest of the school year is absurd, and it's only the first day of school.

9

JASON

We are on line going down to lunch, and I can't resist but take a spot behind Rosie on the line. As I get closer to her, I get this sudden temptation to feel her. I gently caress her back with my palm and feel her every curve from behind. My Rosie turns to look at me, and of course, I have to give her my biggest satisfied smile. I just love her so... NO! My thoughts get interrupted as she starts speeding away from me. I can't let her presence out of my sight, so I keep close to her as much as possible.

Now that I am closer to her than ever, I sniff the scent of her perfectly flawless hair. It smells like sweet Roses, which perfectly suits her name. I brush my fingers softly against her arm and all the way up to her shoulder. There's something about feeling her body that makes me feel so much calmer. The fact that I can touch her is such a rewarding sensation. My eyes roll back, feeling her curves from behind. I can do whatever I want to her because I already claimed her, and she is forever my Rosie. Her smooth milky skin feels so good on my finger pads that are caressing the back of her perfect long neck. I exhale and place my palms on the back of her shaking arms.

Her sweet hair smells so refreshing that I wouldn't mind keeping some hair strands just as a souvenir to remember her forever. That doesn't make me creepy; I'm just very thoughtful of my Rose and her perfect features.

I can't risk extracting her hair shaft just yet, and there's still time for that.

If I could inhale her entire scent, I would without a doubt.

So far, I've familiarized myself with her scent and what she feels like.

Her voice sounds as sweet and smooth as honey. She is just so sweet overall. I wonder if she tastes just as sweet as she appears. I have a big appetite, so I'll save my taste test for Rosie later. Hopefully, once I sit next to her at lunch, I fully enjoy the taste of her precious hands and face. Maybe even tasting her neck and other parts of this perfection wouldn't be so bad. Her body is like a tempting magnet, drawing me closer to her.

Consent isn't needed since I basically own her, and the thought of that satisfies me more than ever.

I don't actually want to eat her... I'm not a cannibal. It's just the nature of a relationship to really get to know your sweetheart on all the deep levels. For me, taste is definitely one of them.

Her entire presence satisfies my senses, but there's so much more to explore on Rosie.

We make it to the noisy cafeteria, and Rosie is already seated at the table. Unfortunately for me, the only seat at the table that isn't taken is the one farthest from Rosie. My Rosie is sitting with hunched shoulders, and it looks like she is trembling. I wish I could be there next to her so I could hold her in my arms. Mark goes on rambling about his pathetic video game stories, and just as I think I wouldn't lose her; Rosie is completely absent from her seat. She can't get away from me that easily, at least not on my watch. Luckily, my Rosie is on the lunch line, and there is already a girl standing behind her on the line. Not to worry though! I can still keep watch of Rosie from behind this girl and still remain in close distance from her.

This really doesn't make sense... just a moment ago it seemed like Rosie was getting school lunch and now she is speeding away with full force off the lunch line. I must go after her to ensure that I don't lose watch of her again. From now on, it's best I stay fully focused on only her... and ABSOLUTELY NO distractions. I got my eyes on you Rosie, and there's no denying that you will choose me unconditionally very soon.

10

ROSIE

I devour the last forkful of buttery pasta and wash it down with the cold water the lunch aids offered to our class. By the time I clean up my space, it is time to leave with our teacher back to the classroom. For a moment, I actually forget that Jason is closely watching me eat the entire time.

We are all lined up, and I can smell Jason's scent getting stronger by the second. As we are walking up the stairs, I feel Jason's body almost entirely hovering over mine. His arms are intertwined around my waist, and I swear I feel like I'm going to lose it. How does nobody notice what he is doing to me? I would try to run away from him, but that's impossible since crowds of classes are in front of me on these stairs. Jason starts humming in my ear as he tickles my inner wrists... I close my eyes to contain my composure and just keep moving forward with my class. How much closer can he possibly get? The smart thing to do is escape now that we are upstairs, but his grip on my upper arm is too strong. Thankfully, our class is just around the corner of the hallway, so this torture should be over soon. I never expected my first day of school to start off like this.

At last, we've reached our front door classroom. Jason's hands finally remove themselves from my body, and I exhale while still trembling.

"Eighth grade, leave your lunchboxes in the classroom because we are about to go to music class."

There is NO way I'm going to leave my lunchbox here after everything I just went through. I hide my lunchbox behind my legs while everyone puts theirs away. The thought of going back into the hallway with Jason touching me makes me sweat buckets. I need a miracle... right now.

11

ROSIE

We are lined up once again going to music class, and I feel a hand pat on my shoulder. I tense up in shock and hope that it's not Jason again. At last, I turn around and there behind me is Tomas, looking at me with a comforting smile. His smile is definitely contagious, and I'm just relieved that it's not Jason for once.

"You seem so happy," Tomas says. Oh my gosh you have no idea. I mean, the relief I feel is intense.

"Yeah, I'm just excited for music class," I respond back.

"Cool and same! Music is literally life. Um, so do you have a favorite music genre?"

"Yeah, I'm into uplifting pop music. Anything that can get me dancing. How about you?"

Tomas's smile beams brighter at my response.

"That is so nice cuz same! I am also obsessed with pop music. I don't have a favorite artist, but I kind of just listen to all pop," Tomas exclaims passionately.

Tomas's approach makes my heart rate regulate at its normal pace again. Maybe today isn't a complete failure after all.

I scan through the hallway, and luckily to my advantage, Jason is distracted, speaking to Mark at the end of the line. I find it easier to breathe and finally loosen up at this fact.

We make it to music class where we are told to stand against the wall for us to be seated in assigned seats. Fingers crossed that I don't get seated anywhere near Jason.

12

JASON

Our class is on our way to music class, and Rosie is not in any near contact with any other boy. In the meantime, I must learn Mark's weaknesses to get rid of him faster. Once he is out of the way, then I will deal with repelling Tomas from Rosie's presence permanently. Here I go...

"Hey Mark, I noticed you were avoiding eating lunch today. Is everything okay?" I say with my most sympathetic tone.

"Yeah, I'm good. I guess I just wasn't hungry. I had a big breakfast this morning."

Mark faces me as we continue walking with our class.

"Oh, that's fine, because I was beginning to worry that maybe you're just allergic to the lunch in school. Are you allergic to anything?"

"Well, I stay away from walnuts because I am allergic to them, but I promise I'm fine. You don't have to worry about me," Mark reassures.

I want to smirk so badly... This is literally perfect. I know one of his weaknesses, which makes Mark vulnerable to me.

"I'm so sorry to hear you are allergic to walnuts."

I couldn't care less that I am being fake to all these bastards. What's important is that I eliminate any potential threats to my Rosie. Getting rid of them seems way too easy, but first I need to make them suffer. I'm going to enjoy this so much.

Oh, hell no... There's no way... Tomas is already grabbing Rosie's attention. Crap! I stayed distracted for far too long.

Before I attempt to stop Tomas, we are already inside of music class. Tomas the turd finally shifts his attention to the teacher instead of Rosie. My delicate Rosie is standing so innocently next to that annoying bastard, which makes my blood boil.

I'm standing against the wall, waiting to be seated in my assigned seat. Tomas is dead if he attempts to spark any conversation with Rosie again. I'm watching them, and I hope Tomas knows that.

Just watching my flawless Rosie, and she is fidgeting with her fingers, probably stressing about something. That's perfect! How could I be so ignorant? I need her to be stressed, so she sees she can't survive without me. She has to crave me and stress over me. I'm tired of our connection being one sided. If she keeps this up, she will suffer very soon along with her pathetic guy friends. This is strike one. The next strike is going to hurt.

13

ROSIE

More than half of my class is already seated, and I'm still waiting to be called on for my assigned seat. Jason is also waiting to be seated, which can't be good. With all my heart, I hope I get seated as far from Jason as possible.

"Jason, your assigned seat is next to Janice. Please sit down to the right of her."

The music teacher looks at her seating chart and then looks back up at me. I had her as my music teacher last year for seventh grade, so she definitely remembers me from that time.

"Rosie, your seat is to the right of Jason. Please take your seat."

My heart just sinks and shattered into a million pieces. This is the moment I've feared the entire time I've been standing in this music room, and now my biggest fear has come true.

Jason is staring at me with his shark smile, waiting to

devour me whole. I can feel a lump in my throat as my eyes tear up. The lights of the room are blinding me with the tears filling up my eyes.

I slowly approach my new seat, and the room goes completely silent. The teacher along with the class are looking at me as though I'm in trouble.

"Rosie, please take your seat. I can't have the entire class waiting for you to sit down," the teacher scolds.

I really don't get how all these teachers lack composure. They get worked up about the most minimal things. I guess it makes sense that slow walking to my seat is interfering with the teacher seating the students. But every second wasted not sitting down next to Jason is valuable. I'm left with no other choice but to sit down now that I am next to my desk and chair. Jason's seat is less than an inch away from me, which makes matters worse. It's been about almost fifteen seconds of me sitting next to Jason, and the walls already seem like they are closing in on me. All I'm certain of is that I've never felt like this before. The classroom looks gloomier when I sit next to Jason. There's that familiar scent I smelled today; Jason is now three times closer next to me than he was a minute ago. I can feel Jason's hot breath on my neck. I close my eyes as hard as I can and count mentally. 1... 2...3... "Hauu," I silently gasp.

Jason is caressing my thigh all the way down my leg. I hurriedly opened my eyes, still shivering in sweat and tears. Jason laughs... it almost sounds like a cackle. His pupils dilate when he looks in my eyes. Suddenly, I notice my lunchbox sitting to the right of my foot on the floor. I swiftly pick it up and place it between mine and Jason's desks while I hide my face behind it. I sit as close to the edge of my chair as I can. I look to the other side of the room, and it seems the teacher is still seating the students down. It's crazy to think it hasn't even been five minutes of class, and it already feels like an eternity.

At that point, Jason's face moves closer to my face as his body shifts closer to mine. I'm about to tip over my chair, but I grasp onto the desk just in time with my sweaty hands. Jason is now taking up both his seat and mine the closer he gets to me. I seriously didn't think he could get any closer, but I was wrong. Why is he doing this to me? What have I ever done to him to deserve all this torture? My sweat trickles down my neck as Jason caresses the back of my neck with his fingers.

Our music teacher is seriously so ignorant. She doesn't even notice everything that is happening with me right now. I can't tell on Jason because that will give him more motivation to torture me. I'll probably also be known as the snitch of eighth grade, so I definitely want to avoid that.

If I had the option to run away from him right now, I swear I would. I doubt I'd even get far enough until he catches up again and invades my space. If he can stop invading my personal bubble and act more human, then I would probably not want to avoid him the way I do now.

Jason continues tickling my trembling arm, and I am so certain that he knows he is making me feel uncomfortable. He just doesn't care.

14

JASON

Music class is over, and we are back in our main classroom. I enjoyed music class so much that I wish it would last forever. I was sitting next to Rosie, and she looked so scared, felt more dominant over her than ever. She deserved to feel that way in music class. That's what she gets for keeping our connection one sided and for trying to run away from me. She doesn't get that I am better than all these losers. In fact, I have something that they all wish they had, power. Once I get home, that's when my work begins, and she will be the one who chooses me no matter how she really feels. She must think I don't deserve her, but at the end of today... I do. Rosie needs to stop denying our love and really open up to me because if she doesn't, then I'll make her. As for the boys, I have something planned for them as well.

Since it's the first day of school, we watch movies for the remainder of the day.

Rosie is sitting far from the boys, which is perfect. But for now, I can relax knowing that I will get my way. Although I am already powerful, I need more power, and that's where my abilities come into play. My twin brother, who looks nothing like me, is the only other person who knows about my psychic abilities. I wasn't born with them, but I somehow discovered them after learning how this universe really works. My grandma is into this kind of stuff, and she was my way of knowing about these powers. Except my grandma has no idea that I have these abilities. Last year, I was snooping around in her room when I came across all her diary entries and notebooks. I read through all of them secretly every night under my blanket with a flashlight, and then I taught myself what she knew. I became a power manifester and got everything I've ever wanted from my parents. I started my own Journal, writing down just a few things that I thought were most important to help me get what I want whenever I want it.

My journal went something like this:

1.) Beliefs create your reality
2.) What you visualize you create
3.) What you fear you attract
4.) What you think/focus on is what you receive/get

... and the list goes on from there. So, I decided that I am ready to test it out. I visualized giving people beliefs and fears that I wanted them to have so I could get whatever I want. All I need to do now is use these techniques to inflict pain into these boys and use my power to mind control Rosie into loving me. In fact, I will make everyone fall in love with me and make everyone treat me like a god. "You deserve the world" is what my parents would always say to me. I controlled them to believe this, and, in the process, I started to believe this myself. After all, life is just a game, and everyone in it is one of my pawns.

As long as I keep up my confidence to use these abilities, I will get Rosie. I will repel these boys, and no one can stop me.

My grandma only used these powers for good (as said in her journals) and there was a section where she would talk about karma. Something about after putting out evil energy and hurting others that same energy would return back to me... in other words I would get horrible karma for hurting people.

Regardless, I couldn't care less because I already know that I can get anything I want because this is my world. There's no point in me fearing karma; karma should fear me. In fact, everyone should fear me because of what I am capable of. Yes, it's true that "your mind is more powerful than you think" – my grandma's journal quote– which is why I have control and power over everyone. It's crazy to think that I hold so much power already, but for all the most obvious reasons, I deserve more power.

15

ROSIE

The school day is almost over, and all we've been doing for the remainder of the day is watching movies. I would rather be writing some interesting narratives or reading a book like we did earlier. I'm still so hungry since I only ate my pasta, and I didn't have time for my turkey sandwich. I'm probably going to finish my school lunch when I get home.

Jason has been staring at the wall instead of the movie the entire time the movie has been playing. He is probably lost in his thoughts again. At least I finally got a break from him. Class ends in a few minutes, so the teacher might tell us to start packing up our belongings. Unfortunately, we have no homework for today, but that won't stop me from writing creative narratives and doing math worksheets when I get home. Education is something that I became passionate about recently, and going to school is actually really fun for me. I just hope Jason doesn't make going to school miserable for me. I aspire to become an author in the future to express my incredible ideas. I believe in myself, so this won't be a hard task.

"Listen up eighth graders, it's time for dismissal, so I need everyone to pack their things and line up at the class door."

As the class is going back to their seats and packing up, Jason is staring at me again with fully dilated eyes and a devious shark smile. I wish he would leave me alone. I've had so much patience for everything I've gone through today, and now I'm glad I can finally go home.

16

JASON

The first day of school was such a success, and it's only the beginning. Now that I'm home, my real work begins, and I'm definitely starting with those guys that were twirling around my Rosie all day. All they've been accomplishing, besides talking to Rosie, is pushing my buttons. Tomorrow, when we are back in school for day two, these boys will feel pain worse than they can imagine.

My twin brother Damien only keeps this secret about my abilities because he is afraid of me, as he should be. Fear is how you get people to do what you want. Without fear, you are undefeatable, and those people are the hardest for me to control. Damien knows that disobeying me would mean he gets punished. He's gone down that path before, and it led him to excruciating pain that I manifested on him. When he and I fight, I always know all his weak spots to beat him harder on. One time, I beat him up so bad that he nearly passed out and got taken to the emergency room, but I didn't care. Damien is deathly afraid of me, so as long as he stays that way, I can continue to control him and have power over him.

Damien was always the confident type of guy who many girls actually really liked. I took that from him, so now all his pride and confidence is mine. I guess it's fair to say that I own him just like the rest of the people in my household. My brother refers to me as a psychopath, and maybe he's right. After all, making people suffer would be a lot harder if I had empathy for them.

My bedroom is pretty plain right now, but I plan to include some chains hanging from the ceiling as decor. It would match my visualizations when I visualize my victims chained up and scared for their lives. That's one of the ways I manifest them to be afraid of me in real life. Somehow it works so well that people tremble at my presence, and I adore seeing how scared they get. They don't know why they feel the way I make them feel, but that's what makes these abilities so much more fun for me. Besides, I can't get exposed because there's no physical proof of anything I do to people.

My first victim is definitely Mark. What he did today is enough for him to be punished. Starting with giving him anger issues and definitely giving him excruciating sensations of fear. He should fear me for what's coming. Tomorrow, I will have him banging his head until he passes out. As for Tomas, I will make sure he gets sick for being such a turd that tries to steal Rosie for me. This is only the beginning. As time goes on, their suffering will only get worse, but now it's time I work on Rosie. After everything she went through today, she still chose to ignore me. My first focus is definitely to stop her development. I can't have her growing or aging because I fell in love with her the way she is now. I don't want her to change, even if she stays looking like a child forever. Next, Rosie has too much patience, and that is a problem because I want the satisfaction of chasing her and actually catching her. By me doing this, Rosie will subconsciously develop a fight or flight response, which will enhance her anxiety. So, taking away her patience is the second step. I also need Rosie to fear me even more than she already does. In doing so, she won't have control over herself because I will control her. Lastly, I want Rosie to love me even if it costs her everything. I know a brainwashing technique that will make her believe that she loves me. As time goes on, I will reformulate Rosie and these boys to my desires. They will be who I want them to be, and they will live life the way I want them to live it. Having control over everything makes me feel unstoppable. Now I just need to wait for tomorrow and watch as all that I've done unfolds.

17

ROSIE

The room grows darker as Jason approaches me closer. His blaring cackle echoes through the room while I scan the area for the nearest exit. There are no doors and no windows.

I try to get up, but something is holding me down. My wrists are chained to the ground, and Jason's cackle grows thunderous as he watches me attempt to escape them.

How did I end up here?

Jason's entire physique expands taller and wider while I'm still stuck on the ground. I try to scream, but no sound comes out.

Defenseless.

There's literally no way out of here, and Jason's shark smile deepens more than ever. I need a miracle right now.

"Get up Rosie," some familiar voice screams. I look around the room, but there's no one other than Jason and me.

"Rosie! You are gonna be late!" that same voice scolds.

My gloomy surroundings fade, and so does Jason. I finally

opened my eyes, and there, standing to the side of my bed is my mom.

"You woke up so late! School starts in less than ten minutes! Get up!" Mom scolds.

I rub my eyes and look up at my digital clock. "7:52" it reads.

It takes a few seconds to process that my dream was just that— a nightmare that I will hopefully forget about once I get to school.

My heart races a marathon and my mouth feels like the driest desert. I've never felt like this before, even after a nightmare.

Somehow, I managed to finish my morning routine and head out for school. I don't have enough time to eat my breakfast bagel with butter, and I'm so hungry. My stomach makes gurgling sounds three times in the car. Thankfully, Dad's annoying radio is too loud for Dad to notice the grumbling. Dad would explode if he found out I skipped breakfast.

School started thirty-five minutes ago, and honestly, I don't mind that I am late. If anything, it's an advantage to me that I get more time wasted on not being around Jason.

As I enter the building, I'm greeted by an entire staff crew surrounding me with cold looks. One of them hands me a late pass and I awkwardly walk past them and head towards my classroom.

My entire class is reading their books, and I'm coming in forty minutes late. Jason looks too occupied with his chapter book to notice that I just came into class.

"Hello dear, it's about time that you finally showed up," Ms. Hendrick smiles insincerely.

"Take out your book and start reading," she says as she snatches my late pass from my hand.

I'm never late anywhere, so this is entirely new to me. It feels weird getting to school way after everyone else got here.

Yesterday when I got home, I was so preoccupied with writing creative stories and sketching my best drawings that I went to sleep later than I was supposed to. Writing fiction is like leaving the real world into a realm of infinite imagination. After everything I'd been through yesterday, doing what I enjoy most was the only thing that could revitalize me.

Jason is looking into his book, but his smirk grows slyer the longer I look at him. There's something so magnetic about him— I just don't know what. It's like something is making me mentally gravitate towards him.

Is he always this attractive?

He looks at me with his shark smile and everything goes blank. My hands are shaking, and my face feels so hot. His laser eyes narrow onto my eyes, and I can't resist but turn away and hide my face behind my lunch box. I can't stop smiling, and my face is probably a tomato. Mark looks at me and then looks at Jason.

"I think Rosie likes you, bro," Mark loudly whispers. Our entire table faces me and smirks.

Jason's face suddenly transforms to the same cackling face from my dream. I wish I could forget that horrendous nightmare and his terrorizing face. I think I'm still traumatized from yesterday, and I'm starting to think it really is just the beginning.

Since I came so late, reading time should be over soon, and we will go to lunch any minute now. I literally can't wait to finally eat something.

I try to distract myself from Jason, so I start a conversation with Mark.

"I forgot my poems at home, but I'll try to bring them tomorrow if you still want to read them," I say while finally cooling down from all the heat.

Mark's hand is in a fist and his face transforms instantly.

"Maybe you should've been more responsible cuz now I

couldn't care less about your dumb poems. Don't bother bringing them to me," Mark exclaims with a heated tone.

What is going on today? Mark doesn't seem like himself at all.

Jason looks like he's holding in the biggest laugh imaginable.

He stares at me harder, obviously on purpose. I hide my tomato smiling face behind my lunchbox again.

Suddenly the room goes completely silent, and everyone's eyes narrow in at Tomas's table.

Tomas's entire desk has his spewed-up breakfast all over it. All of the students that sat next to Tomas are pinching their nose to avoid smelling the stench.

My entire table of kids, including myself, get up and move farther away from Tomas's table.

Jason is the only one smiling eagerly at Tomas. Wow, he is really enjoying this.

"Everybody sit down at your seats NOW!" Ms. Hendrick screams.

We all hesitantly take our seats while pinching our noses. My nose hurts from pinching it so hard, and I have to hold my breath. Jason's eyes travel from me to Tomas and then onto me again.

Luckily, lunch time is starting in a few minutes, so we can all leave while the janitors clean up the mess.

Hold up... where is my lunchbox?

I scan the classroom for any hints of the lunchbox, and there it is laying under Tomas's desk.

How did it even get there?

The last place I left it was on my desk to avoid Jason.

I'm so focused on finding my lunchbox that I didn't even notice that the entire class was waiting for me.

"Rosie, grab your lunchbox and LET'S GO! I don't have time for this," Ms. Hendrick yells... as usual.

"But I can't, it's under Tomas's desk where he—" I say until Ms. Hendricks interrupts.

"ENOUGH! Rosie, I am giving you ten seconds! The class will be late to lunch because of you, so HURRY UP!"

My eyes fill up with tears, and I bend down next to Tomas's stenchy, gooey desk. My butt is visibly shaking as I struggle to pull my lunchbox out from under Tomas's desk. The entire class silently watches me drag myself and my lunchbox out from that nasty desk. Jason is silently laughing, looking at me struggle. I speed walk onto the class line, and we make our way down to the cafeteria. Tomas goes to the nurse's office with all his belongings to get picked up by his parents.

I sit far away from Jason at the lunch table and attempt to open my stenchy lunchbox with Tomas's gut stains all over it. The inside of my lunchbox seems fine, but I'll get school lunch instead. There's no way I'm gonna force myself to eat from that. My mom packed me a baked salmon sandwich and a cosmic brownie bar. This is probably the most appetizing lunch I could've eaten today, but because of the Tomas incident... I can't. Jason isn't in his seat anymore, and I start to smell his strong scent coming from behind me. I shut my eyes and hold my breath as though it will make him disappear.

"Such a shame what happened to Tomas back there huh?" Jason whispers with his hot breath into my ear.

I turn to him, but he's already gone back to his seat as though he didn't just creep up behind me. When the moment is right, I'm going to get school lunch and hope that Jason doesn't come too.

18

JASON

This morning is one I want to remember eternally. Rosie came late today, which is great because her mental suffering is only beginning. Whatever she dealt with this morning must have caused her to come to class later than usual. Seeing the look on Rosie's face when she got scolded by the teacher was so satisfying. If she wouldn't have ignored me yesterday, her suffering would've been slightly more bearable. Watch out, Rosie, this is only the beginning of your worst nightmare. Today, however, my focus is more on the boys that dared to interfere with mine and Rosie's connection. Rosie is still scheduled for suffering today, but lucky for her the boys have it worse for the day. Today is just a warning, but the next time will be worse than hell for them. Rosie has been blushing and smiling at me the entire time, and Mark exploding at Rosie makes it even better. All this makes me feel so powerful that I can do whatever I want and get away with it easily. The best part, though, is when Tomas lost his breakfast in front of everybody in the class. Rosie's reaction was so priceless, and so was everyone else's. Tomas looks so miserable and weak. It's hilarious that I could laugh in his pathetic face as if it wouldn't get me in trouble. What actually bothers me is Rosie's lunch box that's constantly standing in the way. I want her to stop hiding and to finally just run. I need her to develop a severe anxiety response, that way she will always be running from her problems. So, I threw her lunchbox into Tomas's bile under the desk when Rosie wasn't looking.

I also need Rosie weak and hungry for what's coming next.

Poor Rosie had to grab her lunchbox from all that goop, and it's so funny. I love how her adorable innocent face scrunches up at her lunchbox once she gets back up. She's so cute that I wish to caress her milky skin like she's my puppy. For today, my Rose gets a little more freedom while I work on making Mark undergo torture.

Things are gonna get messy soon, and I can't wait to see it finally happen.

19

ROSIE

I speed my way onto the lunch line, but to my surprise, Jason remains in his seat at the table. That's better for me anyways. I'm literally starving. I didn't even eat breakfast, which is probably why I'm lightheaded.

After what seems like forever, I get my lunch tray and walk back to my seat. Today they are serving a plain hamburger and canned pickles. I also picked up a chocolate milk carton and a spork for the pickles.

I'm only three feet away from the table, and Mark runs right at me at full speed. I swerve to the right as fast as I can before he gets the chance to bump into me with my tray.

What the hell is wrong with Mark today? I did nothing wrong to him, yet he's acting so obnoxious and not like himself. Mark gives me a dirty look and gets back up.

"Yo, everyone LISTEN UP! Rosie has a big fat crush on Jason. Go Jason! Go chase her!" Mark shouts in front of everybody.

I flinch at Jason heading towards me and my lunch tray goes flying in the air and onto Mark's clothes. All the pickles and meat from the burger land on Mark's shoes. The half-opened milk carton stains Mark's pants entirely. Before I can notice Mark's reaction, I find myself running as far as my feet can take me. My breathing is insanely rapid, and my heart is thumping so loud that it can be heard from far away. I look behind me, and Jason is walking slower with a tilted head and fully glaring dilated eyes. I must think logically. Where could I hide where Jason can't follow me? The girl's bathroom, of course! Through all the terror and fright, at last I manage to somehow run into the girl's bathroom. To my surprise, Jason follows me inside there. I run into the farthest part of the bathroom and Jason is getting closer and closer. I start walking backwards as he walks slowly towards me to raise the suspense. He's obviously trying to scare me, and for some reason it's working. I just don't get how or why. It's like the closer he gets to me, the stronger fear I feel, and I literally can't control it.

Why can't I control it?

"STOP!" I finally scream. Jason's smirk fades in surprise.

"PLEASE just leave me alone already. I don't like you, and you are seriously so annoying! So just stop!" I say with all my might. My tears sting my eyes and roll down my cheeks.

I feel like I've used up all my energy today, and I didn't even eat yet.

Without another word, Jason walks away in disappointment. I can't believe that's really all it took. I refuse to believe this is the end, though. I probably angered him for all I know. Who knows... maybe he is cooking up an idea to annoy me even more. Either way, I don't care because I am food deprived. I've been starving myself all day, so I better figure out what to eat before lunch is over.

Once I'm back at our lunch table, Mark is glaring at me all

red and tensed up like he's ready to erupt.

Since when is Mark so angry?

Great! My lunchbox is covered in Tomas's guts, my lunch tray is dumped on Mark and the lunch period will be over in minutes. Just when I thought today would be a better day than yesterday... all this happens. What's most suspicious is Jason is nowhere to be seen, but I shouldn't care because I need to eat. I don't want to waste any more time and risk passing out from intense hunger. I never miss breakfast, and I'm not about to miss lunch.

My only choice is to eat what my mom packed me. After all, maybe it's not too bad since Tomas's insides only touched the outside of my lunchbox. I just hope I don't smell bad after touching this vile lunchbox.

This salmon sandwich tastes so juicy and flavorful. Such a shame that lunch time will be over in a minute. Everyone already threw their lunch trays out and I'm the only one eating. I devour every huge bite of my sandwich without leaving a single crumb.

"Everyone line up for recess! We will spend the remainder of the period there," the lunch lady says on the microphone.

Wow, I'm actually surprised that the official lunch period isn't over yet. This means I can still finish my cosmic brownie bar at recess. Hopefully, Jason isn't already out there. I'm not looking forward to seeing his annoying face again.

20

JASON

Everything that has happened so far in the cafeteria is go-ing according to my plan. Mark keeps attacking Rosie from anger, which is great for Rosie being willing to avoid Mark. It's so funny how Rosie dropped her lunch all over pathetic Mark. Mark's suffering doesn't end here, though. What's coming next is proof that I am undefeatable. Rosie shouldn't have avoided me when she had the chance. What's disappointing is that Rosie rejected me when I chased her into the girl's bathroom. She called me annoying and a bunch of other crap that I refuse to believe. I left shortly after her dumb lecture on how she wants me to leave her alone, but now we have bigger problems.

She rejected me. NO ONE EVER REJECTS ME!

The fact that Rosie thinks she is so entitled to avoid me makes me want to tie her to a wall and punch her with all my strength.

Now that I think about it, maybe that's exactly what she needs.

Motivation.

Maybe what I've planned for Mark is a good start for her to realize that I am the only guy that's good for her. In just less than an hour, there will be one less person I need to worry about.

I can't lie to myself that after Rosie rejected me, I bawled my eyes out with my tears in the boy's bathroom. She has no idea what this is gonna cost her, which is what makes this much more satisfying.

Everyone is packing up to go to dismissal, and I'm still in the bathroom shedding tears. Now I just have to wash my face and keep my head held high because what's coming next will be worth watching. Watch out Mark. You're next.

21

ROSIE

The weather is perfect today. It's not that cold, and it's not too hot either. Just perfect. All the kids are running around the school yard playing tag and other running games. I'd rather finish my cosmic brownie bar because somehow my appetite is still really big. I feel like I'm on vacation with no Jason around and being all alone with my appetizing brownie. Mark is running around and laughing with the other boys from our class. I'm glad to see that he is finally happy today. Mark has been a ball of anger since the moment I got to class this morning, and I still don't get why.

"Hi, you're Rose right?" a random girl says.

This girl has curly orange hair that goes down below her knees and her skin is a really pale white shade. Her freckles are what really stand out, though. They're so beautiful.

"Yep, I'm Rosie. People just call me Rose as a nickname. What's your name?" I say.

"I'm Hazel, but I don't go by any nickname."

"Oh, nice name, and I love your freckles by the way."

"Thanks, I used to get made fun of for having freckles. So anyways... I think we are in the same class. You're Tomas's partner, right?"

"Mhm we're partners, and I'm still processing that he wasn't feeling well this morning."

"Honestly me too! I was like so caught off guard when he puked in class," Hazel says with a hint of annoyance in her voice.

I really like Hazel and her vibes. She's so down to earth and easy to talk to.

We are continuing to walk around the school yard, and Mark runs past and lays on the ground a few feet away from us.

"Mark, what are you doing?" I ask curiously.

Mark avoids my question and starts aggressively banging his head against the concrete floor. It's like he is trying to crack his head open.

"Mark, this isn't funny! Stop!" I scream.

He continues to bang his head on the concrete, but even harder this time.

"Mark, please answer us!" Hazel screams with panic in her voice.

Hazel turns to me with concern written all over her face.

"MARK I'm seriously getting worried! Can you tell us what's happening with you?" I shout.

"Rose, I don't think he's pranking us. I think something is happening with him."

Mark's head is now bleeding from the center, and he continues to bang his head on the concrete. His face is completely frozen, as though he has no control over himself.

"MARK, STOP, PLEASE!!! STOP!!!" I cry, tears rolling down my face and my heart racing.

"SOMEBODY HELP!!!! Please somebody call the school

aid!!!" I cry out.

"HURRY, HE IS BLEEDING!! WE NEED AN AMBULANCE!! PLEASE HELP!!" I cry out with all the strength that I have.

What's happening?

Everything feels like a haze, and nothing makes sense anymore.

The school aid comes running towards Mark, who is lying on the ground turning pale and barely moving.

What is going on?

First Tomas... and now Mark??

Moments later, the entire school yard of hundreds of kids are surrounding Mark's body. Jason is standing in the back of the crowd... And he seems happy?

Regardless, that's not what matters right now.

There are three school nurses and an ambulance outside of the school yard. The paramedics are running towards Mark as the crowds of kids move out of the way. They take pale Mark away and drive off hurriedly.

The whole class is sobbing, and I still can't stop crying on the floor that Mark banged his head on. My cousin who I literally just met yesterday is taken away to the emergency room, and there's nothing I can do to help. I hope he comes back, and that he is still alive. If Mark is still conscious, then he's probably terrified for his life. Our entire class is back in the classroom, and everyone is crying... except for Jason. I don't even care that Jason is staring at me with dilated eyes because right now all that matters is my cousin that I really don't want to lose.

"Attention class. I know you are all aware of the incident with Mark. We've contacted his parents and informed them what has happened. Please remain calm. We all want Mark to come back, but crying won't make it any easier."

I can't believe the audacity of the teacher to tell us to stop crying. I mean, how could we? We don't even know if Mark is alive anymore.

We are supposed to go to music class, but for some reason we are still in the classroom. I can still smell the hints of stench from Tomas's accident earlier. The janitors barely did anything about the smell, so this is what we'll be dealing with for the rest of the school day I guess.

22

JASON

At last, the moment I've been waiting for all morning has manifested. An entire crowd of students is circled around Mark, who is probably dead by now. Mark has been banging his head on the concrete floor and poor Rosie is so concerned.

Rosie really cares for this bastard, and that's not okay. The good news is that I have one less idiot to worry about. Rosie can't run to another guy to protect her because these morons are gone now. My lovely Rose has no choice but to stick with me. All I have to do now is keep watch of all the other boys who get anywhere near Rosie. If only she knew all the trouble I'm going through for us to end up together, but it's all worth it.

The paramedics drive away with Mark, and that is one of the most satisfying feelings I've felt all day. It's Rosie's lucky moment because she's next. All this crappy whining about missing Mark is really starting to piss me off. Just accept that he is gone and move on! It's really not that hard. I wouldn't mind killing off Tomas and all the other idiots in this class, but that would be way too easy. I'd rather enjoy their suffering and feel the satisfaction of watching them ooze away into the deepest depths of suffering. It feels easier to exhale just thinking about Rosie's guy friends screaming from pain and torment. I'd totally laugh, though, because that's some entertainment I wouldn't dare to miss out on.

Out of nowhere, some guy, probably in his mid-20s, enters our classroom holding a clipboard in his right hand.

"Hello eighth graders. I'm Coach Gerald, and I am your gym teacher. I just wanted to introduce myself before I bring you to my gym."

This funky-looking tall dude that claims to be our gym teacher doesn't even look fit. I thought gym teachers were supposed to be athletic-looking, but apparently not this guy.

Rosie is so attentive to this dude, and it's making me want to knock that clipboard onto his bald head.

I'm starting to think that clipboard is just a prop to make him look smarter, since he must be such a dumbo in real life. He's wearing shorts that are twice the size of his body, and they look like they'll slip off at any given moment. I hope they do... at least then this guy would be worth watching.

Rosie looks at me with her innocent gaze and then looks away quickly while her cheeks start reddening. I got her! I just know it! Tonight, I need to continue the mind control technique since it's working wonders on my Rose.

If Rosie won't love me naturally, she will have to learn to love me through these abilities. In fact, I want every girl in this class to have a crush on me. Maybe this is how I get Rosie to be jealous over me. I need girls to chase me, so she feels guilty for ever ignoring me. I got eyes on you, Rosie, and any fool that interferes with our relationship will go down to hell very soon.

23

ROSIE

I'm still trying to avoid the nasty stench coming from To- mas's desk. The good news is we get to leave this class to the gym any minute now.

The skinny man, who appears to be our gym teacher, thinks it's a good idea to introduce himself here... in the very class that still stinks horribly. I'm usually very patient, so having this great need to get out of here is new to me.

Our class is lining up, and I go to the back of the line where hopefully Jason doesn't see me.

For some odd reason, Jason is nowhere in clear sight. It's like he's become invisible all of a sudden, and I honestly wouldn't mind that. If he were actually invisible, I would find peace with that and not grow scared about him touching me at random.

There's that same strong familiar scent that seems to constantly linger around me once I get on line.

Jason.

Obviously.

I let out the heaviest shaky sigh and continue moving forward with our class line. My heart rate paces at its peak as soon as his fingers brush against my back.

When will this end?

It's only day two of eighth grade and it feels like month two.

They say 'time flies when you're having fun,' while for me it's like time is frozen.

Jason's finger digs in between my armpits and that's enough for me to lose it.

"AHHH STOP THAT!!"

All heads turned to my heated face with concern written all over their faces.

I can't believe I actually lost my patience in front of the entire class. I was never like this...

What is going on with me?

I'm known as the most patient girl who always keeps her composure, but what I just did was beyond embarrassing.

Jason's shark smile widens, and he softly laughs but clearly holding in the biggest laugh of his life.

"Excuse me! WE DON'T SCREAM LIKE THAT IN SCHOOL!! Am I clear?" Ms. Hendrick hollers.

Ms. Hendrick's veins are sticking out from the side of her neck...

Clearly, she's the one that needs to calm down. If anything, I have more patience than her.

"Yes, I understand," I say softly, looking down at my feet.

"Now explain to me why you felt the need to scream and scare everyone on this line!"

Oh, my gosh... Can this be the moment I expose Jason?

But what if all this dramatically turns on me?

Jason is unpredictable, but I can't tolerate him any longer.

Here I go...

"I'm sorry. I... I didn't mean to be disruptful. It's just that Jason keeps touching me and making me uncomfortable," I say with innocent puppy eyes.

Jason looks like he is literally going to erupt any second. His face is a boiling hot red color, and his overly dilated eyes are staring deep into my soul.

"Jason, step off the line. You and Rosie will report to the principal's office right now!! Do you understand?" Ms. Hendrick points to the other end of the hallway that says, 'Principal's Office.'

"The rest of the class, follow me to the gym!"

Ms. Hendrick leaves with our class, and I'm left standing a few feet away from Jason.

I speed away with all my might to get to the principal's office as soon as I can.

Jason takes his time, taking the smallest baby steps to reach the principal's office. He looks like he is about to spew his lunch all over.

Wow, Jason is much less intimidating in this state. For the first time today, I feel stronger than ever. This could be the moment that Jason backs off.

It looks like he is holding something in his mouth and trying to hold it in as best as he can.

At least now he can't do anything to me! In fact, I think the principal can really protect me from him.

It's about time we are both standing in the principal's office. It's no wonder students are so terrified of getting called into here. The dark gray walls and the scent of strong hand sanitizer gives me the chills.

On the table in the middle of the room there's a sign saying 'Principal Morgan.'

All these years of being in this school, and I never once knew our principal's name.

Principal Morgan has this cold, dead fish stare. It's like

she's looking right through me when she's looking directly at me.

So far, we've been standing in complete silence, just staring at each other.

Can this get any more awkward?

Principal Morgan is holding a long wooden stick and approaching Jason closer with squinted, intimidating eyes. She slams the wooden stick on the table, making a huge thud sound.

She sighs, "Ah Jason, I've spoken to your mother earlier today before hearing you are in trouble. Wouldn't it be such a shame to ring her back up and tell her you're misbehaving?"

Jason's skin goes completely paper-like pale. It's like he forgets how to speak all of a sudden.

I don't blame him, though. Principal Morgan's intimidating calm tone gives me goosebumps. I only get goosebumps when I'm cold, but it's not even the slightest bit cold in this room.

"So, Jason... answer me. Are the allegations true that you have been touching Rosie?" Principal Morgan fidgets with the wooden stick as though she is preparing to smack us with it.

Jason swallows really hard and says,

"Absolutely not. I have no intention of touching girls without their consent. It's just that I seem to bump into Rosie a lot on the line. She walks so slow."

WHAT... I can't believe him right now. I literally speed away with all my might when he is behind me on the line.

"NO! Principal Morgan, he's lying! He touches me all the time, and he laughs while he's at it!" I shout.

Jason makes puppy eyes, appearing innocent.

"Why would I do that? The teacher would've noticed and said something if I touched you."

Jason pretending like he is the victim is so incredibly annoying.

"THAT'S BECAUSE YOU ARE TOO SLICK TO TOUCH ME WHEN NOBODY'S WATCHING. YOU ARE SUCH AN EVIL, CREEPY PERSON, AND..."

"That's enough, Rosie!! Shame on you for raising your voice like that!"

Jason smirks as Principal Morgan shouts at me. I'm shocked... I can't believe I just lost my patience again. I NEVER raise my voice like that, ESPECIALLY in public places.

"Jason made a good point that somebody would've noticed and said something. So, Jason, you are free to go back to class, and Rosie I need to have a chat with you."

Jason smiles, showing all his teeth.

"Thank you for understanding, Principal Morgan. You don't have to get Rosie in trouble though," he says cheerfully.

"Why is that Jason?"

"Because I'm sure Rosie just wanted my attention. Everyone's been talking about how she's totally crushing on me. I wouldn't want her to get in trouble for obsessing over me too hard."

Oh, my gosh... this jerk did not just say that. HE IS THE ONE THAT'S OBSESSED WITH ME... I just want him to leave me alone. I never asked to be involved with him in the first place.

Principal Morgan side eyes me.

"WHAT? Principal Morgan, Jason is the one that's obsessed. He doesn't ever leave me alone! He starts to stare at me. And I don't understand why he is so annoying. How could I ever like someone like that?"

Jason covers his mouth, chuckling.

"Alright, Rosie, that's enough. Both of you go back to your gym class. If I hear about this drama one more time, you will both be suspended. Understood?"

Jason and I nod our heads and awkwardly walk out of the office door.

Well, that wasn't helpful at all. What was the point of Principal Morgan being involved if she didn't even try to solve this problem. All she did was threaten to suspend us.

Why didn't principal Morgan believe me anyway?

Jason is such a manipulator... and I shouldn't have lost my temper. I'm so confused because I literally never lose control of my emotions.

WHAT IS HAPPENING?

This is horrible. Now I for sure can't complain to the teachers about Jason. The last thing I need is a suspension because of him.

Jason and I are still walking down the hallway in complete silence. I'm trying to avoid eye contact to avoid any conversation with him. I want absolutely nothing to do with him.

Gym is just a few doors down, so this awkward walk with Jason will be over any second now.

24

JASON

Rosie has got some nerve exposing me like that to Principal Morgan. She has no idea what I'm capable of, but now there's no point in going easy on her. Today she proved to me that she hasn't suffered enough. This entire time I've given her a chance and even protected her from the other guys. But after what she did today, she must be punished. No excuses.

She has set me off more than any one of her dumb guy friends. I already know that I'm going to enjoy seeing her misery come into play. Once she's learned her lesson, maybe then she will stop pushing me away and accept that we are meant to be together. I'm tired of waiting around for her. It's about time for me to take action to reel her in some more. Oh, my dear Rose, this is only the beginning. It's funny how she thinks she can be free of me just by complaining to the principal. It's gonna take a whole lot more than doing that, my love.

Seeing her face get all heated when I said she's obsessed with me was so satisfying. Obviously, it's not true, but if I work on her some more, it'll be a permanent fact. There's no point in her trying to get me away from her because, as we both know, I'm undefeatable.

The amplified background chatter draws away the attention from mine and Rosie's appearance at the gym. Our classmates are playing some unfamiliar active games in groups of two.

"You are just in time! Your class is finishing up our fitness game and they are about to start a new one with their partners," the weird bald-headed gym teacher shouts over the background noise.

Rosie and I make eye contact, and she quickly averts her eyes.

"Since everyone already has a partner, Rosie, you can be partnered with Jason from now on."

Rosie's face has panic written all over it. That's perfect! She needs to fear me more than ever. As I get closer to her, she flinches so hard, and it's the most adorable thing ever. It makes me feel so powerful that I know she has no chance of fleeing from me now.

"Boys and girls, the next activity we will be doing is called Tag Down. You will play regular tag with your partners, but once you've been tagged, you do five pushups and tag your partner back. Your partner is allowed to correct your push up position and coach you to do it correctly. You can begin the game."

Rosie is not looking that well right now. I didn't think her milky pale skin could go any paler, but I thought wrong. Rosie flinches before I get the chance to even say anything. Her breath comes in short gasps as her feet escalate in rapid motions through the gym. Meanwhile, I'm chasing after her,but of course taking my time. It's best if she gets a head start to run so that her fear spirals within her stronger the more I approach.

I use my technique to visualize her fear getting stronger the closer I get to her. The fear I gave her is so strong that she might just pass out from the high intensity. I've never given anyone fear to this crazy high extent, so there's no telling what could happen to her next. She deserves to be punished, so after this, she better stop avoiding our connection. I can imagine she feels that feeling I get in my stomach on the roller coaster, and I love seeing her like this. Her face resembles those traumatized girls seen in horror movies running from monsters. The more scared she is, the more power she gives me over her. I visualize her adrenaline coursing hard through her veins. Her breathing is so rapid, I can hear her gasping for air, but she's pacing even faster. Keeping my breathing steady, I push harder and go faster. My Rose is finally slowing down, clearly giving in from all the tension of running from me. Her trembling legs give out and she drops down in the middle of the gym floor; a thin layer of sweat covering the nape of her neck. Rosie's eyes shut slowly and soon our entire class is surrounding her. There's so much commotion going on, even the teacher is in clear visible panic.

"SOMEBODY CALL THE NURSE!! Is she still breathing?" someone screeches.

"Maybe she's dehydrated? Does anyone know what happened to her?!" another shouts.

"Is she alive?" shouts the girl, with tears rolling down her face.

The shouting and questioning from everyone grows louder and more annoying.

When everyone faces away, watching the nurse pace into the gym, I swiftly stomp on her fingers as hard as I can, leaving red marks. Her hands have my dirt shoe pattern marks all over them, so I kick them to shake off the dirt. Once she's awake, she should see her red marked fingers as a warning to not go against me ever again. Stepping hard on her delicate fingers feels so relieving. I would stomp harder some more, but the nurse is already here. In fact, I should've drenched her in more pain as revenge for snitching on me. Maybe digging my nails into her precious skin would be a better way to add to that warning. She still hasn't been through enough suffering, but for now this will do. I'm such a generous guy for stopping her torment here. I could've done way worse, but I'll save that for another day if she disobeys me again. If I had more time, I would make her bleed, but not to the point of killing her. I wouldn't kill my love for disappointing me, but rather hurting her is more satisfying.

"Everyone step back!" the nurse carrying Rosie cries out.

The nurse that's wearing disposable gloves puts her on a bed with wheels and the other nurse pulls her away. I'm surprised they didn't call the emergency room like they did with Mark. I'm sure she's not dead, but the whole class freaking out makes it seem as though she is dead. All of our classmates are pacing around in commotion and others are crying like they just lost a loved one. Such a shame Mark isn't around to suffer seeing his dear cousin passed out and in pain. That's alright though. Mark is dead, and that's good enough for me.

"Attention class. I know that today has been very hard for all of you, but please bear with us. We are taking you all outside for the remainder of gym time to play. Rosie will be okay. She just needs to rest, but she will be back soon," the annoying gym teacher screams over all the roaring cries.

Everyone is crowding out the gym doors to go back outside, but I have plans of my own. I'm off to the bathroom because what I'll do next is something I should've done a long time ago. Rosie should be back soon, which I'm not worried about. I just need to make sure she will be around in the next ten minutes to witness what's coming. Everyone is outside by now, but I'm in the boy's bathroom. I can't wait to do what I usually do at home. My best chance is doing it here where I can focus. I want to put every girl I've seen in our class under an obsessed love spell. ESPECIALLY my lovely Rosie. I need crowds of girls chasing after me like they are paparazzi, and I am the celebrity that everybody likes and desires. I need girls fighting for me and Rosie getting jealous for my attention. I'm using my favorite technique from my grandma's journal, so there's no way this plan could fail. All I have to do now is step outside where everyone is playing and watch as my doings manifest into reality.

25

ROSIE

There's a blurry sight of an entire crowd of heads circled around, looking down on me. All their faces blur away as my eyelids give out and shut. Next thing you know, I'm lying on a hard, leveled, high surface.

Where am I?

The strong scent of alcohol and hand sanitizer hits my nose abruptly.

"Nurse Molly! She's awake," a girl with an ice pack on her knee calls out.

The woman, who I assume is the nurse hurriedly runs to me with an orange juice box and crackers. "Oh, great you're awake. How are you feeling sweetie pie?"

I try to sit up, but it's like my head outweighs my body.

"Lightheaded," I respond.

"Here, drink some orange juice. It will help you."

I sip the over-sweetened orange juice from the mini straw and strangely enough notice red painful marks on my fingers.

My middle, index, and pinky finger hurt so much when I try to bend them. I don't even remember how I hurt my fingers.

"Sweetie, do you remember what happened before you passed out?" the nurse says, patting my leg to be comforting.

"The last thing I remember was I felt scared, and I was running and then I started feeling lightheaded, and it's like my vision was blacking out a bit. Next thing you know, I was on the floor, and now I wake up here."

"Alright honey, why were you feeling scared?"

She places a wet cloth on my forehead and makes a pitiful face.

"My partner Jason was chasing after me because we were playing tag, and I've never been so horrified in my life. I don't know what happened, and I don't remember how I got these marks on my fingers."

The nurse nods her head sympathetically as I speak.

"It could be dehydration that made you feel this way. Have you been drinking enough water?"

"Yes, I always stay hydrated. I don't think I was dehydrated."

I elevate myself up and try to stand. The first few steps are wobbly, but I am getting the hang of it.

"I will call one of your parents to inform them of what happened and that you're feeling better. Do you think you can go back to class now?"

I nod my head and pop a saltine cracker into my mouth.

"Okay Sweetie, if you need me, I'll be here in the nurse's office. Take your belongings and orange juice with you."

The nurse hands me a pass. "Your class is outside."

"Thank you," I say as I walk out of the nurse's office.

Today has been the weirdest day. First, Tomas got sick in class, then Mark was taken to the emergency room and now I've just woken up from being passed out. I don't know what's going on, but I'm starting to question the safety of our class.

I get that Mark's situation is a mystery. But why'd I pass out? I didn't think that being so petrified of Jason would get me to this point. All he did was chase me for the gym activity, but it felt traumatizing when it wasn't supposed to.

Is it weird for me to think Jason is behind all this?

I know it may seem impossible, but Jason seems to get suspiciously happy when something sad happens. Maybe it's just because he's naturally a psycho insane person that thinks it's funny seeing someone in pain, or he's behind all this damage. Regardless, I have no proof, and I'm still not entirely certain he did anything.

I'm finally outside, and it is like a jungle out here. Jason is running around in front of a huge stampede of girls chasing him like they're a bunch of hyper excited obsessed puppies. Jason seems to really enjoy it though. His shark smile reaches to his ears. He keeps laughing like he's having the time of his life. I catch his eye, but he ignores that I just got there and keeps rushing around full of joy. Jason seems so attractive it's actually crazy. I can't believe I haven't noticed how cute he really is. He's got the prettiest laugh, gorgeous eyes, and everything about him is so breathtaking. Aside from the fact that him chasing me earlier took my breath away... literally. Either way, I'm glad he's finally busy. I can relax and be at peace for once today.

I hear someone whining not far from where I am standing. I turn around and there's Hazel bawling her eyes out against the school fence. I approach her as fast as I can.

"Hey Hazel, what's the matter?"

"NO WAY. Oh, my god... Rosie? I thought you were gone for good. How are—"

"Yeah, but I'm okay," I interrupt.

"Why were you crying?" I asked, hugging her in sympathy.

"Well, for one, I was worried about you, and it's about everything that's been happening today. It's been hard to take in and process it all."

I let out a deep sigh and sit down beside her on the fence.

"Trust me, I'm just as confused as you are."

"You know what makes it all worse? Jason has been completely ignoring me. One of the girls chasing him threatened to punch me if I went near him," Hazel weeps.

Her tears roll off her chin, and she wipes them with her sleeve.

"I can't help that I'm attracted to him, but ignoring people is so rude," Hazel raises both her arms.

Hazel's tears roll off her chin and onto her sleeves. Her eyes are puffy, and she's sniffling hard through her red nose.

"Oh my gosh. You like Jason?" My voice fades.

"Yeah, literally every girl is crushing hard on him right now, which sucks. I just wish he wouldn't ignore me."

"Pfft believe me when I tell you, I wish he would ignore me."

"What? You're kidding, right? He's the cutest, most popular guy ever. Any girl would be lucky to get his attention," Hazel raises her voice in defense.

"Well, not me. Jason may be strangely attractive lately, but he's so annoying. He always touches me and chases me. I'm literally petrified of him."

"Maybe you're just a spoiled brat, Rosie. I'd kill to get that attention from him. You're lucky I'm the only girl you told this to."

"Mhm why though?" My face is puzzled.

"Are you kidding? If any girl finds out what attention he gives you, they'll attack you out of jealousy," Hazel cries.

Hazel has both her hands in fists.

"And you won't?"

"Of course not. I wouldn't be mad at you unless you actually liked him back, so you're safe with me."

Oh crap. I think I really have feelings for Jason. I don't

know why, but I'm somewhat attracted to him. Why all of a sudden though? After everything he's put me through, this is how I feel about him. I'll have to keep that a secret from Hazel. That doesn't change the fact that he's still a creep, so I should stay away from Jason at all costs.

These girls that are all over Jason remind me of chihuahuas. It's like they're his dogs, except they don't have a leash attached to them.

Maybe all this female attention Jason is getting is for the better. The busier he is, the less I have to worry about him disturbing me. I've been through enough hell already.

"Oh, and Rosie, I'm so sorry about Mark," Hazel pats my shoulder.

I can't do this anymore. I slump down into a ball next to Hazel. Tears are blurring my eyes and rolling down the sides of my face. Today was overwhelming, but I get the feeling this hell isn't over yet. Now Hazel and I are weeping together. I cover my face with my sweater to hide the crying.

I wipe my pinkish nose with a pocket tissue from my sweater and sniffle.

"Mark didn't deserve what happened to him," I say.

Hazel zones out in the distance.

"At least you came back feeling better," she says.

I force a smile. The thought of Mark being gone makes me shiver. We haven't heard any news about him since the tragedy happened. I don't think he'll be back. It's been too long and still nothing. No good news. No reassurance. Nothing.

The gym teacher blows his whistle, and our class crowds the entrance to get inside the school.

Gym felt like it was taking an eternity to be over. So much happened in such a short time frame.

Hazel and I are behind our class coming inside the building.

"Yo Hazel!" a girl from our class shouts. "Stay away from

Jason! If you don't, then expect to get a good beating at dismissal." Her friends cackle hysterically.

Hazel nods speechlessly.

"Good girl. I know you'll make the right choice," the mean girl says in a high-pitched voice.

"Amelia, I already told you I don't like him like that," Hazel says with a shaky voice, looking down to her feet.

Amelia cackles, "Yeah right! You cried over him during gym. Admit it, you can't resist him, but just know that Jason is too good for you. Jason is mine! Let's go girls, Jason our lord is probably waiting for us inside."

"Lord? Seriously?" I whisper to Hazel.

"Yep. They praise Jason like he's a god. I'm not surprised, are you?"

"Of course I'm surprised. I understand if they are crushing on the guy but praising him that hard... yeah no. That's really extreme," I say with certainty.

I can't believe this. They are LITERALLY treating Jason like a god, which is insane. Since when? Today has been full of surprises, but out of all of them, this one is the strangest. Why all of a sudden?

Jason is just a regular person... a totally attractive person... But still! Why put him on a pedestal? Am I the only person that's not buying this? Something's definitely going on, and if someone doesn't put a stop to it, there's no telling who's next to get hurt.

26

JASON

I had the BEST time ever during gym. I wish it would've lasted forever. Every girl was in love with me and literally fighting over me. I can't resist but adore all the attention I'm getting from everyone. It was one of my favorite parts of today. Rosie's best friend Hazel was crying over me like a desperate, sad little girl, which I loved. It felt so empowering, and the best part was I ignored her and watched as her self-esteem crumbled right in front of me. Gym felt like a vacation full of so much satisfaction, except for one thing. Rosie is the only girl that didn't chase after me or obsess over me. I don't understand... I forced her to artificially be in love with me, but...

WHY THE HELL DOES SHE STILL NOT CARE? It makes my blood boil just thinking about Rosie being the only girl that doesn't obsess over me.

Why is that?

I got every girl to like me so effortlessly, and now they see me as their god. However, something is still standing in the way of mine and Rosie's connection. I thought that getting rid of Mark and torturing Tomas would solve the problem. But all it did was give me satisfaction. It didn't bring Rosie any closer to me. I thought that making Rosie jealous would work, but she didn't care one bit.

What if I work on getting rid of every guy in this class overall?

That would work, but it would take too long. I need to do something that will put all these worries at ease. I need Rosie to only strictly focus on me. I think I know what I must do.

Since we are back in class, we will be leaving for dismissal at any given moment. This is my chance to plan out how I can follow my Rosie home. Maybe Rosie has other interests. I need to get rid of so that I become her only interest. She should be praising me and loving me because that is her purpose in this world: to serve me and fulfill all my wants. Since this is my world, I get to choose what happens and when. I never liked the idea of religions because people would waste time praising someone that wasn't me. I deserve all the praise simply because I deserve everything I lay my eyes on. Rosie is my biggest desire, so it doesn't make sense why she isn't fully in my grasp.

Right now, we are writing stories as an assignment for our reading subject. We've been writing for almost an hour already.

Has the teacher forgotten about us?

The only topic I could think to write about is Rosie and my mission to follow her home. I won't actually write about that and risk getting caught; I'm not stupid. I know it sounds stalkerish and creepy following her home, but in my defense, I'm just being a romantic. There's nothing wrong with being curious about the person you love. I know I'm doing the right thing and for all the right reasons. Rosie needs to accept our love, and if she doesn't, then I'll be left with no choice. If I can't have her, then no one can. I obviously wouldn't kill her. I would have to find a way to keep her locked away from any guy who desires to be with her for as long as she lives. It sounds impossible, but I'm a master at plans. I attempted locking away my first crush in an abandoned soundproof garden shed when she chose my brother Damien over me a few years ago. Everyone thinks she's dead, but really, she's been living in that shed for almost two years now. I remember when I controlled her family's search party to not want to look for her and throw them off track, making them believe she's dead. I can't have anyone helping my prisoners escape.

It's hard kidnapping a girl all on my own, so I did what I do best and used my abilities to make it easier on myself. I planted intrusive thoughts in her head to make her willing to get into the sketchy shed. This technique took almost all my energy since I had to see where she was at all times to make sure she walked in the right direction of the shed. I followed her from her house to where I intended to keep her held captive. She instinctively knew where the shed was thanks to my directions that I gave her through her thoughts. It wasn't easy, but it worked so well. People are never seen walking anywhere near the shed because that's exactly what I want. Of course, I did this to her out of love and to protect her from anyone who could potentially steal her from me.

I bring her leftover snacks and water once in a while, so I'm not that cruel. I wouldn't just let my first love die. I'm very generous for even bringing her a huge round garbage dumpster to do her business in.

Of course, I would only do that to Rosie if I really ran out of options on keeping her in my grasp forever. For now, I should stick with my first plan of learning some more about her outside of school. What makes this plan even harder is that my mom picks me up from school today. I'll figure it out though; I always do. Rosie is sitting across from me as usual, so focused on her writing assignment. I'm not surprised though. She said it's one of her biggest passions. I feel so tempted to feel her once more, but I have to hold myself together and not blow my cover for later.

"Boys and girls, finish up your last sentence because we will have some people share their stories. Any volunteers?"

Rosie's hand shoots up in the air so rapidly before anyone's can.

She's sharing her story, and I just realized how cool it would be to have her voice be my alarm every morning. I know it sounds weird, but her voice is so soothing that it can put me to sleep. I guess it wouldn't be the greatest idea to have her voice as my alarm in that case. It puts me in such a meditative state. Her voice is as smooth and sweet as honey. I can listen to it all day like it's music to my ears. I may not be able to touch her, but hearing her makes up for it.

An applause from the entire class breaks right into my thoughts.

"Wow Rosie! You are so creative, and your writing skills are very impressive. You should write your own book one day!" Ms. Hendrick says with a joyous tone.

"Thank you. I hope I write a book sometime. It's something that really interests me."

AHA! How did I not realize earlier? She is interested in writing, which is something I should remove from her. I need to start removing her interests one by one as much as I can until there's nothing left but me in her eyes.

Her passion and happiness are in my way, so that's gotta go, too. Right now, I'm jotting down in my grandma's journal a list of things I need to remove from Rosie so she can be completely mine with no interference.

Some other people have shared their stories, and no one clapped for them at all. Wow, so Rosie really does have a huge talent for being a writer. Such a shame that will be taken from her, but she has brought this upon herself, so it isn't my fault.

I gave her multiple warnings, which she completely ignored. Maybe I should've stomped on more than just her fingers. I'm too generous to her. I should've been a lot harder on her even after everything she's been through. This isn't over.

Our class is all packed up for dismissal and my delicate Rose is waiting for someone to pick her up... and there's my mom approaching our class to take me home.

"Mom, I forgot to tell you. Uncle Jerry said he would pick me up and I would hang out with him for the day. He said he's parked at the main entrance of the school, so I'll just walk over there myself."

"Okay, I'll say hi to him then."

"NO... NO, it's okay. You don't have to do that! ... Um, Uncle Jerry said I have to hurry up because he is in a rush," I say, trying to sound convincing.

Mom gives me a skeptical look.

She sighs, "Fine, tell Uncle Jerry to bring you back home before dinner time."

Mom leaves... finally. I thought she'd never leave me alone. Meanwhile, Rosie's dad is already leaving with Rosie, and I'm still back here with my class. I catch up to Rosie, keeping a distance behind them.

NO! They aren't walking home by foot. They are getting in Rosie's dad's car! There's no way I can catch up with them, running after a car without getting caught. I guess my only option is somehow getting inside the car with them.

Rosie's dad opens the trunk of the car and takes out a snack from the snack box then gives it to Rosie. They just got in the car and the trunk is automatically closing slowly. I swiftly squeeze into the trunk before it closes shut, and we are on our way to Rosie's house. I haven't thought about how I'd get out of here yet, but that won't matter until later.

"Ah, you like the walnut cookies too?" Her dad says.

"Mhm, how could I not? They're my favorite!"

Interesting. Rosie likes walnuts. Might as well give her a walnut allergy. I can't have her liking anything but me... even the most minimal of things in life. By the time we are out of the car, if she has another walnut cookie, her allergies that she doesn't yet know of will act up.

I'm so lucky I can keep a better lookout on Rosie like this. That way, I can find more ways to gain full control over her life. I should be the one choosing what she consumes, what she does, and how she feels. Basically, I must control everything there is possible about her. My sweet Rosie has no idea what I'm doing to keep our connection alive and stronger than ever. If I won't fix her to my liking, then who will?

"Dad, turn on some pop music. The type I love to exercise to."

"Right on it!"

How have I not thought of that? I can't have her growing and developing, so I should without a doubt remove her desire to work out. The slimmer and shorter she is, the better. I want her to stay looking the exact way she did when I first fell for her. I already put a stop to her development before, but making her not want to exercise is a great addition to this.

"Yes, we're here! There's seriously no place like home. Today was crazy, Dad. I'll tell you all about it when we're inside."

Oh, no... they're leaving the car! All I have to do now is crawl into the driver's seat, unlock the door, and walk out.

Now that they're out, I'm about to catch up behind her, but what I completely forgot about is shutting the door. What if closing the door is too loud and they notice I was in the car? I have to make a run for it.

On a count of 1... 2... 3... I shut the door and run, run, run! I'm so out of breath now, but I can't stop now. I've made it so far. Literally... I ran all the way to Rosie's backyard.

Rosie's huge window is entirely open, and there she is

brushing her hair right next to it. She is not looking directly out her window, so she can't see me. There's probably a mirror dresser next to her window. I can sit here and watch her all day, but that's not why I'm here. I need to take note of everything that makes her most happy and get rid of it through my techniques.

Rosie just stepped away from her window, which has to mean she left her room, right?

There's a really long hose in her backyard, so if I just throw it into her window and attach it to something so it doesn't fall, then I could get in her house and continue my mission there. It's kind of hard learning about my Rosie from all the way in her backyard. I grab the hose that's lying next to her lemon tree, and I attach it to a sharp claw thing lying around. I honestly don't even know what that is, but it can help me get into Rosie's house if it's attached to the hose.

I throw the end of the hose-claw contraption, and now I just have to climb. I'll leave my bookbag next to the bikes, but I'm taking my grandma's journal with me. I'll need it for when I control Rosie and take notes of all that I've learned about her.

I take a deep breath.

I'm ready...

I grasp onto the rope with my left hand and then my right and I repeat that.

Crap! I didn't realize there was a beehive at the right side wall of Rosie's house. This is gonna be a lot harder than I expected. There's already a swarm of bees flying in my direction.

I'm losing grip of the rope and there are bees buzzing next to my ear to make matters worse. My twin brother got stung by a bee and got taken to a hospital because he was allergic. What if that's the same case for me?

I'm now dangling on a hose halfway up Rosie's house, and there's no way down now unless I...

"AAAAAAHHHHHH!!!" land directly on the Roses with the

spikiest thorns. My shriek is so loud, I just know somebody heard me.

"Dad, did you hear that too? It's coming from our backyard."

CRAP.... Rosie is gonna come into the backyard, and here I am tangled in the thorny rose bush. OUCH it hurts so much. I feel like a thorn is stuck onto my knee. Now that's what I call torture. This is probably karma, just like it said in my grandma's journal, but that won't stop me from getting Rosie where I want her. Karma doesn't scare me... In fact, Karma should be afraid of me instead!

NO!!! To make matters worse there is a camera in her backyard pointing to me the entire time. It's fine... I mean it's not like they check their camera every day. I'm gonna be in so much trouble if I don't get out of here right now. I'm shaking as much dirt off myself as possible now that I am out of the bush. Rosie's voice sounds closer, which means she's going to be in her backyard any second now.

What sucks is this entire time there was a backdoor that was open the whole time! I could've at least got inside through there. Rosie is coming, so I grab my backpack and run. Hopefully Rosie gets an allergy reaction now so I can buy myself time to flee her backyard.

I run as fast as my feet can possibly take me. My legs feel like giving out, but I push myself harder even through all the soreness in my knees. I have to find my way home, which sucks. This street isn't familiar at all.

I feel like I'm forgetting something. I just don't know what. I mean, I have my bookbag.

HOLD UP... my grandma's journal! I dropped it in the bush thorns when I fell down off the hose.

I can't go back now. It's too late. To make matters worse, I forgot to take down the rope from the window. I wouldn't have enough time anyway because I would get caught even faster. I have to find my way home, and my entire outfit has dirt marks all over it. How will I explain this to Mom? Worst of all, how will I get home now?

I thought I had this plan under control, but now it's a horrible failure that might just get me exposed. I can't run anymore nor can I take another step. I drop down to my knees on the right side of the sidewalk. I need to take a break before going again. My stomach is making sounds, obviously indicating how terribly starving I am. I hadn't eaten or drank at all today and I don't even know where I am. My eyes feel stung by my tears that are racing down my cheeks. What have I done?

At near distance, some concerned feminine voice calls out.

"Jason!" it calls.

The voice grows louder the closer the person approaches me from a distance.

It's hard to tell who's calling out my name from the tears blurring my sight.

"You are in so much trouble! How dare you lie to your mother!?"

My mom runs up to me and bends down to my level that I am slouched sitting on.

"Do you have any idea how worried I've been about you? Or this is some joke to you?"

Mom's voice intensifies in roaring rage.

"Let's go, we are going home. NOW!"

She pulls my sleeve and shakes me aggressively.

I am gasping for air through my intense weeping. I can't gather the energy to say anything, so I weep louder instead.

Mom stands up and sighs heavily. Her arms are crossed, and she faces away from where I am sitting curled up into a trembling ball of misery.

"I called Uncle Jerry, and he said he wasn't with you today because nobody informed him to pick you up!"

I finally speak through my clogged nose."Mom, no, you don't understand. I really did think Uncle Jerry would pick me up today."

"ENOUGH WITH THE LIES ALREADY! You are just like your father. Always lying your way out of situations. Why can't you be more like your twin, Damien? Damien is well behaved and makes smarter choices."

Mom covers her face with her hands in annoyance.

"YOU ALWAYS COMPARE ME TO DAMIEN!!! Am I not good enough for you? Do you even love me? You were always there for Damien, but you don't care about me." My voice fades, and I'm bawling harder than ever. It's true. Damien is all my parents care about. Mom gives him so much love but looks at me like I'm a disappointment.

My mom doesn't display even a single bit of sympathy on her face.

"Get up and get in the car! I don't want to hear from you right now, Jason."

My legs tremble as I am forcing my body to stand up straight. Some dirt on my clothes shakes off.

"You've got dirt all over your clothes! Where the hell were you?"

"I thought you didn't want to hear from me, Mom."

"Don't even dare talk back to me! I am your mother!"

"No, you're not. I don't see you as one anyways."

Mom gets silent in complete shock, staring at me.

Without another word, we are driving home in complete awkward, tense silence.

All that's occupying my mind is my grandma's journal in Rosie's backyard. If she finds it, then I'm doomed forever. All I wanted was for Rosie to choose me willingly, but what I got in return is a cold shoulder. I'm not done yet. There's still work to be done, and Rosie is mine no matter what anyone thinks!

27

ROSIE

Today was the craziest day of my life. I'm glad I'm finally home because now I can destress from all the crap I went through. My dad doesn't know that I passed out today, but it's better I don't tell him. He's already got enough on his plate, and the last thing I need is for him to worry about something that's probably not even a big deal. Dad already found out about what happened to Mark through Mark's dad, and he is devastated. He doesn't show it, but I know what he feels is painful. It's painful for everyone, especially for myself. I was just getting to know Mark, and this had to happen to him. What doesn't make sense is that I passed out the same day as Mark, yet he was taken to the hospital and I wasn't. How did they know my situation wasn't as severe as Mark's? I mean obviously what happened to Mark was dangerous since he was uncontrollably banging his head on the concrete. At this point, all I can do is hope a miracle happens, and that Mark comes back.

I'm brushing my hair, which oddly always helps when I am stressed. I can breathe easier now, which is a good sign. I just stepped away from my room and some loud shriek and bang sound came from my backyard. I can't help but feel like that sounded like Jason's voice. I could just be paranoid at this point, which is understandable after everything that happened today.

"Dad, did you hear that too? It's coming from our backyard," I call out to dad.

"No, I'm shaving right now. I didn't hear a thing. Is everything okay?"

"I hope so. I'll check out what happened in the backyard and I'll let you know."

"Okay Rosie. Just be careful!" Dad shouts from the bathroom.

I slip my feet into my pink sparkly shoes, and I storm out the door.

I chew on a walnut cookie to calm myself, since it is my favorite snack. For some odd reason, I feel like my throat is closing up and my hands are becoming a pinkish color.

"What the heck?" I shriek in concern.

I spit out the walnut cookie all over the floor and rush inside to get water.

It feels like it's getting hard to breathe, and there are bumps around my lips.

"Rosie, what's happening to you!?"Dad shouts.

I chug water from my water bottle, unable to speak. My throat feels itchy all of a sudden.

"I think you're having an allergic reaction, Rosie. Here, take this with water."

Dad hurriedly hands me an allergy pill. I've never taken a pill before, but I've seen people take it before. Without hesitation, I place the pill on my tongue and quickly chug my water so fast that I nearly choke. I feel slightly relieved even though my throat is still itchy, but hopefully the pill will help that fade.

I take a deep breath and sit up on my couch.

"What am I even allergic to?"

"It depends. What was the last thing you ate?"Dad says, sitting beside me.

"I felt this way after eating a walnut cookie, but this doesn't make sense. I had them in the car and I felt perfectly fine."

"Well, now it's best you don't eat them for some time to be safe. Did you see what happened in the backyard?"

"Nope, I was about to, but the person probably got away by now because my allergy reaction gave them a head start to flee."

"Don't worry about it. We have a camera system where we can check out what happened there. I'll pull it up on my computer in the basement for you," Dad reassures.

We are at my computer set up in the basement, and I've never felt so desperate in my life. I really need to know who was in our backyard. I just want to be convinced it isn't Jason so I can be calm for the rest of the day. Honestly, me assuming that Jason was in my backyard is so absurd. I know he is really annoying and creepy, but I doubt he would take it this far. There's no way he would follow me home. Right? Dad pulls up the recorded video from our camera and oh my gosh. THERE'S NO WAY MY SURREAL THEORY IS TRUE. Jason was dangling off a hose leading to my bedroom window. I don't even know what to think anymore. My legs feel like giving out again just like they did before I passed out earlier.

"Now who the hell is that kid? Rosie, do you know him?" My Dad's voice fades and mumbles away.

My reality looks warped and distorted and everything becomes black. My head outweighs me and I start laying back, losing control of my legs that have lost any ability to function.

Ice cold water smacks my face, and my eyes open wide. I

am rapidly gasping for air, and my senses are slowly coming back to me. After what seems like the longest minute of coming back to myself, my dad stares at me with worry, holding an ice jug of water.

"Rosie, can you hear me?" Dad cries out.

"Yeah Dad. I'm okay."

I sit up from the floor, attempting to sit up without my head outweighing me again.

"I think you had a panic attack, Rosie. Has this ever happened before?"

"Yes, actually... today in school—"

"ARE YOU CRAZY? And you didn't think it's important enough to tell me?" Dad yells. His head is in his hands.

"I'm fine, really. Just please show me the camera footage again."

"No way. I don't need you passing out again!"

"Dad, just please trust me. I'm prepared this time, and I won't pass out. This is important, and I need to see the footage as soon as possible."

Dad looks at me in sympathy and sighs. He pulls up the footage, and there's the replay of Jason climbing up to my window. For once, the beehive on our house was actually useful. The bees attacked Jason, and he fell into our Rose bushes. But... he had something with him.

"Dad, replay his fall again."

I watch the replay again and notice that some purple notebook Jason was holding fell with Jason into the bushes. Only Jason didn't leave the bushes with the notebook, which means it's still in the rose bush right now. Jason left all the evidence behind, and now I actually have raw footage of him attempting to break into my house. Ugh, he is such an obsessed psycho freak. Whatever delusional fantasy he is living in his twisted mind, I want no part in it. I'm still trying to understand how he managed to follow me home... unless he was in my dad's car too. I'm surprised I'm somehow still sane after all that's happened today. I passed out twice in one day from panic, and now I am certain this isn't for no reason. I have to get to that journal.

"Rosie, this is crazy. Answer my question: do you know that boy?"

"Yes, Dad, but I don't have time to explain. I have something to do."

"Excuse me? You better start speaking, or I will call the cops on this boy."

NO! Dad can't call the cops, or it will ruin everything! I could use this footage to blackmail Jason into leaving me alone. I can't let Dad expose Jason! The last time I did that, it backfired terribly. Even though we have evidence this time, I can't let my dad interfere, no matter what. I'm not taking any chances.

"Dad, replay the footage. You'll see that Jason dropped something in the bush and left it there by accident."

"So what?"

"Maybe this belonging of his can tell us something we don't already know."

"Rosie, this is ridiculous. What if it doesn't?"

"Then we'll find another way, but for now please don't make things worse than they already are."

Dad sighs and raises his voice. "I don't know what's going on, but I need to pick Mom up from work right now! DO NOT leave the house for your safety. Okay?"

"Okay, Dad, don't worry about me. I need to get to my homework anyway."

Dad leaves to get Mom from work, which buys me some time to get that notebook from the bush in our backyard.

I slip into my shoes and leave the house to my backyard. The hose is still dangling from my window and many rose vines and thorns are damaged. Behind the bush is Jason's purple notebook. I pick it up and brush off the dirt from the cover with my fingers.

The notebook looks very old and many of the pages inside look like they've turned yellow and stiff. A huge portion of the book has neat script handwriting and many pages at the end of the book have sloppy handwriting. Clearly this notebook belonged to two people, and I'm intrigued to see what it says.

It's been almost an hour that I've been reading through this notebook, and I feel like my entire reality just got flipped upside down. It's like everything I've ever known is a lie, but it all makes sense now. I've read enough to know how this universe really works, how Jason was the reason for all the damage, and how I need to stop him. I really don't want to believe all the stuff he wrote about me here and how he potentially killed Mark. He tortured everyone for me, but most importantly, he made me suffer the most. I hate to be the reason for what happened to Mark. The thought of it makes me want to drain my eyes out with tears. Turns out that this is Jason's grandma's journal and Jason used her secrets and abilities to hurt everyone.

All I have to do is fully understand how he did it so I can undo it.

Overall, I highlighted the main points in this journal that I think stood out most:

- *What you believe becomes your reality*
- *What you fear you attract*
- *What you allow will continue*
- *Your mindset affects how people treat you*

What stood out most is 'what you allow will continue,' which makes so much sense! I never stood up for myself when

Jason would torture me. I let him abuse me when I could have told him off.

'What you fear you attract.' I feared Jason more than I feared anything in my life, and according to this journal, when you fear something, you give it power and attract it more. Even though he forced this fear onto me, I let it consume me, and I should know better than that.

The journal also said that "What you give attention to gives it power." Jason is clearly really power hungry, which makes sense why he is so desperate for my attention. He wants power over me, but if I avoid giving him attention, then there's no chance he can obtain that power.

Ugh! My dad will be home soon, so I need to study this as fast as I can before he gets here. Jason doesn't stand a chance because now I know his tricks. As long as I play my cards right, he won't get to me.

Finally, 'Your mindset affects how people treat you.'

Hold on, what is a mindset? I hurriedly go inside and search on a nearby computer in the basement.

"Mindset."

According to the internet, the mindset is, "A person's way of thinking and their opinions."

Basically, it's a combination of what you believe, what you think, and how you see yourself.

I skim back to the journal to the part where it is says, "What you believe becomes your reality."

So this entire time, I saw myself as the victim WHICH IS WHY I got treated like a victim. I BELIEVED that people try to control me, WHICH IS EXACTLY why that actually came true.

So basically I got treated this way and attracted all this crap because of my thinking. My bad beliefs and my bad thoughts manifested all this Jason drama. I attracted someone like Jason because I had a belief that I attract controlling people, plus I saw myself as a victim.

Now that I know that 'beliefs create your reality,' I need to change my mindset as soon as possible before I attract something that will make me suffer again.

Phew... oh my gosh all this gave me clarity, but if there's one thing that's clear for sure, it's that this was all my fault too.

- *I allowed Jason to torture me without standing up for myself.*
- *I feared Jason, which attracted him to give me more fear in the long run.*
- *My mindset attracted all this to happen in the first place.*

Plus, if I wouldn't have seen myself as a victim, I wouldn't have been treated like one.

I go to the last page of the purple journal, and I start writing.

"The Plan"
Step 1: *Change the way I see myself. I want to see myself as someone who is very popular and has many friends.*
Step 2: *If Jason tries torturing me again, I DON'T ALLOW IT! Stand up for yourself because "What you allow will continue."*
Step 3: *Change my beliefs. Self explanatory. Just change my mindset the way I want to be treated.*
Step 4: *Start believing that all the beliefs that Jason gave me don't control me anymore, so everything he has done to me will be undone.*
Step 5: *Stop fearing Jason because when you give something attention, you give it power, and what you fear you attract.*

"Rosie, we are home and we brought pizza from your favorite shop!" Mom calls in glee.

Perfect! For once I'm not worried about school tomorrow because I am about to make some changes to my mindset. I am so over Jason, and by knowing that, I can relax and eat my pizza in satisfaction. I won't allow Jason to control me anymore because I am taking my power back.

28

JASON

This morning my whole family avoided speaking to me at all. Mom must have told them about our fight from yesterday, but at this point I don't care.

I'm sitting across from Rosie as usual, and she looks happier, which can't be good for me. After what happened yesterday, I've tried giving Rosie beliefs to avoid going into her backyard– unless it's too late and she already found my journal there. Mark's seat is completely deserted, so I don't mind sitting closer to Rosie to replace that brainless dead bozo. My sweet Rosie has been glowing in joy ever since I got here. I have never seen her looking this calm, and it bothers me. Our connection has been completely one sided, even after all I've done for her. I've protected her from threats, and I've been keeping my eyes on her since day one, yet she still chooses to give me the cold shoulder. After moments of casually and innocently relocating myself, I finally find myself in Mark's seat. It feels empowering replacing the one idiot who tried stealing what's mine.

Rosie has been so focused on writing her paper that she doesn't display any reaction now that I'm sitting next to her. Usually she would tremble at my presence or even flinch when our eyes meet.

Why has she changed all of a sudden?

Suddenly, our class is facing the front door, looking like they've just witnessed the greatest miracle humanly possible.

No. There's no way. I refuse to believe it. Mark is back? I would hope Mark's ghost came back, but instead comes back the most irritating human to ever exist in this world. What happened?! I thought I got rid of him for good.

With all the commotion raising, I lose my train of thought.

"Settle down everyone! This is Mark's twin, Anthony," Ms. Hendrick calls out.

Sudden silence breaks out and everybody freezes.

Mark has a twin brother?? I had no idea, and Mark never cared to ever bring him up. Anthony looks entirely identical to Mark, which is horrible news. If Rosie liked Mark, then couldn't that mean she would like his identical twin too?

Rosie's eyes are fully enlarged and desperate. She's probably hoping to hear that pathetic Mark survived.

"Hi everybody. I'm here to tell you that Mark is alive and recovering, and he will be back soon, but he wanted me to personally deliver two of you a note," Anthony says.

He pulls out two red small papers and quickly glances at them.

"The notes are for Rosie and Tomas," he announces.

Why would this freak ask his twin to hand deliver his notes? If he is obviously alive, then why not just give the notes to them himself?

The fact that Mark wrote a note to two of my victims is most definitely suspicious. If Mark knows something that he's not supposed to know, I have to make sure he stays gone, and this time undeniably.

Rosie and Tomas have their hands raised, and Anthony delivers them the notes from Mark.

"Thank you, Anthony. You can go back to your class now," Ms. Hendrick says through her warm smile.

Anthony leaves... finally.

I place my hand over Rosie's hand before she begins to open her note. She is obligated to share what's in that note unless she would rather I find out myself.

I squeeze Rosie's hand harder and show my brightest smile.

She looks up at me, alarmed. Good, I've got her attention.

"Jason, you are making me uncomfortable. Would you quit touching me?" Rosie says in a provoked tone.

I quickly take my hand away. Wow, Rosie has really upped her game. I can't let her speak to me like that. I OWN HER! Has she forgotten??

"I wouldn't speak to me like that if I were you." I lower my tone and stare at her intensely to intimidate this ungrateful girl.

"Or what? You'll torture me the way you tortured my friends? You'll stalk me? That's right, I have the video footage of you climbing my house, and unless you want that video exposed, I suggest you leave me alone."

She smiles sarcastically and continues writing as though nothing happened.

Our entire table of four is now staring at me like I've just crapped myself. I'm lucky that the whole class didn't hear what Rosie just said, but these four look curious in ways that can be dangerous to mine and Rosie's connection. I still can't believe that Rosie stood up to me so suddenly. The last thing I need is being exposed for what I've done. I don't see myself as a stalker, but simply a protective person. But people won't understand that. This whole time I've been protecting my Rose, and now she dares to talk back to her authority.

She embarrassed the crap out of me, and now there's no telling what these kids think of me. Or worse, they might reveal my secrets to the rest of the class. Most importantly, nobody knows about my abilities, so I should be safe for now.

"Rosie, I don't know what you're talking about, and I really don't mean to bother you. I just really care about Mark because he's my friend. That's why I simply want to see what's in that note."

I make my face look as convincingly sympathetic as I can.

So far our table of students look relieved and not as skeptical of me, which is perfect.

"I can read between the lines, Jason. You are no friend to Mark."

Crap! Where'd Rose build up all this confidence from?

"Just open the note, Rosie. I know you want to."

"Or what? You'll put a spell on me and force me to show you the note?"

She definitely read my grandma's journal. This makes her dangerous to not just my reputation but to our connection that I so desperately tried keeping alive.

Joke's on her. It seems like the kids at our table are laughing at her. Probably thinking about how foolish she sounds. I guess exposing me won't be so easy. I chuckle with the rest of the table to make her feel small, because that's what she deserves for talking back to me. Watching as Rosie's self-esteem shrinks and gets torn to shreds feels greatly empowering.

"Haha, yeah I know I'm so hilarious," Rosie chuckles with us.

All of a sudden, everyone's faces transform into adoring faces.

How is that possible??

Within just seconds, Rosie's confidence strengthened, and it's like our table sees her to be cool again. I miss one minute ago when we all laughed at her for about ten brief seconds.

Now her mindset changed so suddenly.

"Rosie, you are truly so funny. I love it!" someone from our table said eagerly.

I don't get it... Rosie wasn't even being that funny. Why is everyone loving her so suddenly?

Ah, right! She changed the way she thinks! If only the mindset portion of my grandma's journal was never there, then she would've never learned how to improve herself.

Now that Rosie has mastered confidence and changing her mindset, I can't keep our connection lasting any longer. Too much is at stake here. My abilities and my history with all these victims is strictly something I can't have exposed. Worst of all, I hate that I can't hurt Rosie anymore. Punishing her with excruciating pain would satisfy me, but that would get me exposed. I can't control the one person that I love so dearly. What will I do now?

Rosie finally takes a quick glance inside the folded red note. Then she quickly looks at Tomas, who is already looking at her, and they both nod in sync.

It's like they are both part of some plan and they are signaling something to each other.

"Rosie! I'm so relieved your cousin is better!" Hazel chirps from behind us.

"I know right! I can't wait to see him again."

Hazel giggles and side hugs Rosie.

How could I be so ignorant? I missed out on such beauty and only now I'm noticing.

Hazel's got this voluminous curly orange hair that kind of reminds me of a lion's mane. Her sky blue eyes call out to me,'I'm all yours,' and I welcome that. I can imagine how smooth and sweet her skin must taste. I can almost feel it just by watching it glow so clear and textureless. I caress her hand gently and she looks down at me sitting.

"Oh hey Jason," she says casually with the most clear angelic voice.

I found my soulmate. My one and only. My Hazel.

She walks back to her seat and I nearly melt in awe. The way she moves so flawlessly. I can watch her for days.

Rosie and I could've worked perfectly, but I needed her to see me as authority, which she disobeyed. Now that she's so confident, torturing her feels almost impossible. Lucky for me, I got Hazel now, and soon she will be wrapped around my finger desperate for me. Hazel is weak, which is exactly who I need. Someone who doesn't have the inner strength to overcome me is what I love to see. When I watched Hazel cry once I used that love spell, it showed that she has been my most loyal victim all along. I need her to be willing to be tortured for our love.

This is only the beginning of our love story, and one I won't give up on. Rosie may not be my focus for now, but that doesn't mean I won't keep my eyes on her... forever.

29

ROSIE

For the first time since the first day of school, I feel so un-leashed from Jason that I feel like I can freely fly, denying nature's laws. I feel like I can do anything. I'm glad Jason left me alone, but now he's got eyes on another. Poor Hazel has no idea what she's going to experience, but this isn't my battle anymore, so I'd rather stay out of it. I can't risk getting involved and getting hurt again. The best thing I can do for myself is continue building myself up so high that Jason won't be able to reach me. Before Hazel came up to me, I opened Mark's vague note. I reread it four times already, and I really don't know what to expect.

It said:

Jason did it. Don't believe me? Meet me around 'Gresty park' with Tomas after school.

Thankfully, today was a peaceful, regular day. Jason stopped torturing me, which feels like such a relief. Hazel, on the other hand, is going through it. During recess, Jason has been chasing around Hazel, who looks terrified,but she acts like it is no big deal after a while. She trembles and sometimes cries when Jason is around her, and ugh, I remember how excruciating that felt. Nothing new really has happened besides Jason torturing someone, so yes, today has been a normal day.

I didn't get the chance to talk to Tomas yet, but now that we are at dismissal, we should be meeting up with Mark soon anyways.

Dad comes to pick me up, and we leave the school and get into the car.

"Dad, can you drop me off at Gresty Park? I'm meeting up with my friends there. You can wait for me in the car if you want."

"What friends? Is it that kid that climbed our house? If it is, then there's no way I'm letting you meet with him."

"NO. NO, Dad, trust me, he's the last person I'd ever want to meet up with."

"Okay, well whoever these friends are, be careful!"

"Of course, I always am."

We arrive at Gresty Park and there's Tomas, Mark, and another boy I don't recognize standing with them. I get out of the car and run to them as rapidly as I can.

"Hey Rosie, you're just in time," Mark says.

"OH MY GOSH MARK!! You're okay!!! What happened to you?"

"Jason happened."

"I don't understand," I say, acting as though I'm clueless.

"Don't worry about it. You will soon. But for now, Tomas and Rosie, meet Damien. Jason's twin brother."

Wait, what? Jason has a twin? Yet they look nothing alike. Not even one feature of their face is the same. Damien actually looks really attractive compared to Jason.

"Woah, but you look nothing like Jason," Tomas says,

completely thunderstruck.

"Yeah, I know. Everyone says that. Um, so anyways, we invited you here today because—"

"Hold on. How do you and Mark know each other?" I interrupt.

"Oh right, So we met at the hospital. Mark was there because he nearly died, and I was there because Jason beat me till I nearly couldn't breathe or function anymore. We shared a room there, and we spoke, and now we're friends."

"Wait but how—"

"Stop! No more questions," Mark exclaims.

"We have important news, so just chill for a minute," Damien says abruptly.

"Now, here's what I want you to do. You see that shed over there?"

Damien points outward. Tomas and I nod.

Damien hands Tomas a key.

"I need you to open that shed."

"Why, what's in there?" Tomas asks.

"Just open it and you'll see!"

We all walked over to the garden shed and a revolting scent of feces hits my nose as we approached the shed closer.

We all cover our noses with our shirts, and Tomas turns the key.

The shed door opens and there, sitting tied up on the floor in the middle of the shed is a malnourished looking girl around my age. Her clothing looks like it's turned to rags, and it smells like she hasn't showered in years. She looks up at us with hopeless eyes. Around her there are tons of mini snack wrappers and a huge garbage dumpster, which I assume is where the gross smell is coming from. That must be her bathroom. She looks so miserably tortured.

"Please help me!" the girl cries.

Tomas gasps while his alert eyes meet mine.

"OH MY GOSH! It's... It's..." My voice trails off. I feel a huge lump in my throat, and my eyes sting from tears. The girl is trembling in fear, unable to move her tied down legs. Wooden rope with strands of fibers sticking out is tightly looped around her knees and ankles. Her wrists are tied conjointly together by thicker wooden rope.

"It's okay, don't worry! You're safe now," Damien says in a reassuring tone.

My legs feel stiff like they are frozen inside of huge ice blocks. I can't believe what I am forced to process right now.

"Tomas, you untie her wrists, and I'll untie her knees. And Rosie you untie her ankles."

The rhythm of Damien's breathing has sped up.

"Mark, you keep a lookout at the entrance in case Jason appears."

Mark does as he is told without another word.

"Damien, I know this is a bad time, but who is she?" I ask.

Damien sighs as he attempts to undo the wooden knot that's tied around the girl's knees.

"That's Emma, Jason's first crush. He found some way to lock her in here for years."

I rise up at full speed and cross my arms.

"How could you! THIS ENTIRE TIME YOU KNEW ABOUT EMMA AND YOU LET HER SUFFER IN HERE?" I yell.

Tomas looks completely pale and unable to speak. Tomas's trembling fingers are still struggling with freeing Emma's wrists from the rope. Droplets of sweat are racing down his neck.

"NO, of course not! Jason would always take our leftover snacks from home and bring them somewhere. He refused to tell me what he did with them, so I followed him here one day."

"You didn't even think about telling an adult about this?"

"Um... AND RISK MORE LIVES? How could I? Jason can

control people with his mind, and I'm not interested in going up against him again."

"NO! Please, I am begging you. Don't let Jason find out you helped me!" Emma cries with terror in her voice.

Emma continues whining and crying hysterically.

"Don't worry, Emma. Jason won't do anything to any of us. You just have to trust me."

Damien frees her knees and takes over my task of freeing her ankles.

"You could've helped her escape earlier! Why wait for us?" Tomas shrieks.

"Because I didn't know where the key was but I told Mark about this hostage girl, and after we got discharged from the hospital, I eventually found the key in one of Jason's desk drawers. I wanted to let her out, but Mark wanted the both of you to see this too."

"Why...?" Emma asks through her sniffles.

"Good question," I add. "Why Mark?" I keep my arms folded and pout to express dissatisfaction.

Tomas, who finished freeing Emma's arms, looks back up at Damien furiously.

"I don't want to make you feel more endangered and panicked than you already are but... In Jason's new journal, he's written plans on kidnapping Rosie once he finds a place to keep her."

"Just stop! HOW DARE YOU? You sociopath. Have you got no empathy? You planned on keeping this information from me, which can put me in danger!" I exploded.

I shove Damien, completely disregarding that we are in the middle of saving Emma. But this is far worse since I could be next.

I can't believe I just lost control again. I would never lay my hands on anyone, especially from anger. This has to be because of Jason, since that's all that makes sense to me at the moment.

Damien is frozen in disbelief, just staring back at me until he finally speaks.

"I get that you're upset and I... I honestly believe you have every right to be, but... don't take it out on me! Do you understand?"

"What confuses me is why you didn't tell any adults?" I say, throwing my hands up in the air.

I can tell Tomas, Emma, and Mark are very uncomfortable. They are staring at us in silence, not knowing what's next.

"I can't risk my brother finding out because the last time I told on him, he punished me through his mind-controlling abilities."

Tomas tilts his head, looking puzzled at Damien.

"Tomas, I get that you're confused, but it will all make sense when you read my grandma's journals," Damien reassures.

Tomas nods his head, still skeptical, but changes the subject.

"Why Mark? Why do you care about us?" Tomas asks while he buries half his face in his shirt. Surprisingly I got used to the stench, but Tomas clearly hasn't. I'm more concerned with my safety than caring about the nasty smell.

"It was the right thing to do. I mean we were all in this together. We were all victims of Jason's abuse. We just didn't know it."

"What do we do now?" I say.

"Help her, obviously!" Tomas screams in annoyance.

"Duh, but how?"

"No, no, don't worry about it. This is my brother's problem, so I will fix it. For now, take my grandma's journals."

"Huh? What do we need them for?"

"Just read them and all will make sense. They will help you overcome all the torture you've been through. All I ask is PLEASE DO NOT expose my brother! If you do, then there's a chance we will all end up like Emma, for sure."

"Wait, but Jason is thirteen years old. How did he manage to do this and get away with it?" I ask.

"I honestly don't know. I'm still trying to figure it all out, but for now take the journals and act like none of this ever happened. I can locate Emma's parents."

"But what will you tell her parents?" Tomas questions.

"Don't worry about it. I'll know what to say."

"Tomas, you okay?" I pat his shoulder.

"Uh um, yeah, I think. Just processing this all."

I'm back home and I'm still trying to process all I just witnessed, but it will be okay. From all this craziness, I learned a lot. Enough to write a whole book about it. Even though being involved with Jason has been complete hell for me, I'm still grateful to him. This is the strongest I've ever been in my life. I heard somewhere that 'life doesn't become easier, you just have to become stronger.' Jason helped me become stronger through everything he's made me go through. I'm sure that applies to the rest of his victims. If I choose to stay mad at all he has put me through, I'll waste away a life where I can be happy and enjoy all the great things about being here. Jason impacted me so much that one day I will write a book on our crazy story to teach others how I learned to become stronger. I will name my book Eyes On You Forever, except it won't be forever after all.

ABOUT ATMOSPHERE PRESS

Atmosphere Press is an independent, full-service publisher for excellent books in all genres and for all audiences. Learn more about what we do at atmospherepress.com.

We encourage you to check out some of Atmosphere's latest releases, which are available at Amazon.com and via order from your local bookstore:

Icarus Never Flew 'Round Here, by Matt Edwards

COMFREY, WYOMING: Maiden Voyage, by Daphne Birkmeyer

The Chimera Wolf, by P.A. Power

Umbilical, by Jane Kay

The Two-Blood Lion, by Nick Westfield

Shogun of the Heavens: The Fall of Immortals, by I.D.G. Curry

Hot Air Rising, by Matthew Taylor

30 Summers, by A.S. Randall

Delilah Recovered, by Amelia Estelle Dellos

A Prophecy in Ash, by Julie Zantopoulos

The Killer Half, by JB Blake

Ocean Lessons, by Karen Lethlean

Unrealized Fantasies, by Marilyn Whitehorse

The Mayari Chronicles: Initium, by Karen McClain

Squeeze Plays, by Jeffrey Marshall

JADA: Just Another Dead Animal, by James Morris

Hart Street and Main: Metamorphosis, by Tabitha Sprunger

MEET THE AUTHOR

Julianna Pinkhasova was born in New York City and is about to graduate her senior year of high school. When she's not writing, she produces creative and comedic scripts for potential film sketches. Aside from her interest in film making, Julianna highly enjoys studying human psychology.

CPSIA information can be obtained
at www.ICGtesting.com
Printed in the USA
LVHW100751250223
740366LV00007B/548

9 781639 888016